# THE LAST OF HEAVEN
## by
## Martin G. Elster

*My thanks to Susan, Paul, Vivienne, Nigel*
*and Lady Lisa for their help and inspiration.*
**M.G.E.**

Copyright © Martin G. Elster, 2016
Published by Elster Publications, London, 2016
ISBN: 978-0-9935300-0-5

Typeset in Minion by Bopcap Book Production, Manchester.

# Contents:

*Book One*

# MISS PERFECT

Timeframe: 1978-79

When you do dance, I wish you
A wave o' the sea, that you might ever do
Nothing but that, move still, still so,
And own no other function.

*The Winter's Tale*

# I

WHILE THE ROMAN FAITH persists there will always be convent schools like St Margaret the Martyr, catering for intelligent and well-groomed girls of the middle class and upwards. The sisters who run the school are by and large well-attuned to the modern age, and guide most things with a liberal and practical hand; necessarily so, perhaps, because St Margaret's is a boarding school, set in a remote part of the West Country, and vigorous girls between the ages of eleven and sixteen should be allowed their heads from time to time. But ultimately, of course, the commandments must prevail, and those few caught disobeying them are dealt with, regretfully, by Sister Helena Thomas, the school's popular Headmistress; and if necessary they are even expelled. "Benign but firm" is the motto, in accordance with the school's conception of its Heavenly Founder.

A few decades ago, when the affluent invested generously in education, St Margaret's had reached a high-water mark of expansion and prestige, boasting almost three hundred girls and a new science block. This latter did not enhance the view of the old chapel nearby and vexed some of the more traditional sisters. But it was a sign of the times, and signalled the subsequent appointment of male staff to teach the newly established sciences. One or two of the men were presentable and under thirty, and Sister Helena regarded their presence as a bold demonstration of her faith in human as well as divine goodness – not to mention her desire for higher academic standards. Her big achievement was to bring about these changes while preserving the character and the élan of the nineteenth-century School. Many proudly declared that its true Golden Age was the present.

Virtually all the girls of St Margaret's made good progress and achieved high standards, both at the School and in later life. For entrance, there were of course minimum requirements of wealth and ability, but as in all schools the intake varied a great deal in quality, encompassing a wide range of talent and temperament. There were, for example, girls like Annabel James, born leaders, mature and responsible, plainly destined to succeed in every field of endeavour from the academic to the athletic. Then there were girls like Pauline Potter, shy, tense, secretive, born outsiders, creatures whose few successes were modest and hard-won. Whatever the material, St Margaret's did its very best to develop potential and encourage ability, within the broad outlines of the creed to which it owed its allegiance and its existence.

This is a story about two girls who, one strange spring afternoon, strayed well beyond those outlines.

Let us dwell further on the two names above. First, Annabel (who was usually first). She was of medium height, robust and athletic in build. Her movements were brisk and uninhibited, and had distinguished her on the hockey pitch and the tennis court. Her mind was quick and efficient, untroubled by excessive imagination, and capable of much concentration. She began to excel in the sciences when she reached the fifth year at the school. She spoke the Queen's English agreeably, and her manner was a pleasing blend of deference and jauntiness. Clean of limb and stout of heart, the straightest of shooters, she was everyone's first choice for captain, prefect or monitor. Nobody more perfectly epitomised the spirit of St Margaret's. Second, Pauline (who was "too often content with second-best"). She was tall and thin, an awkward combination of fragility and harsh angularity. She struggled at hockey (Second Team), was very good at art and muddled through everything else. She was unattractive (coarse sandy hair in unwholesome curls, yellow teeth, a constellation of pimples on either cheek) and decidedly unpopular, but because she was capable of vicious ill-temper when provoked, she was not bullied. Many believed she was a little mad, and kept well away. The nick-names of the girls indicated their standing among their peers. Annabel was known affectionately as "Jamey"; Pauline, derisively, as "Potty". Annabel took little notice of nick-names; but Pauline bitterly, quietly stored the venom in her sting.

Both girls were approximately the same age. Both were in their fifth, final year at St Margaret's when, on one remarkable day, tails became heads and second became first.

## II

PAULINE, LIKE EVERYONE else, knew all about Annabel, who had put a hand on most of the prizes of recent years, both sporting and scholastic, but it was only during this last year that they were together in the same form and Pauline was able to perceive her at closer range. For most lessons, both girls sat in the back row of desks, Annabel among her gang by the side wall, Pauline a few desks away in the middle of the row, sometimes with her one or two casual acquaintances. Her first impression of Annabel (following initial disgust when "Jamey" had been loudly elected Form Captain) was one of smoothness, of streamlined *finish*: not just the manner, but something about the physique suggested the perfection of a gleaming machine. With her artist's eye, Pauline observed the details as the weeks of the Autumn Term went by: the thick dark-brown hair, parted in the centre and falling elegantly to the shoulders; the healthy honey-brown complexion; the bright tawny eyes, the straight nose (with the slightest of upturns at the tip), the shapely cheeks, the full-lipped mouth, the finely pointed chin; and the calm and steady expression, demure and ladylike, which would relax frequently, delightfully into the most winning of smiles. Very often Pauline's concentration would lapse during lessons and she would doodle in the margins of her exercise book. She found herself, time after time, scribbling cartoons of grinning mouths, until she realised that she had been trying to recreate Annabel's smile. She couldn't, though, because the smile was all motion, a magical energy of movement: the quick and easy rhythm of the upper lip, disclosing hard white teeth with the utmost charm and confidence, was something that no artist's pen could reproduce.

There were other details, however, which caught Pauline's eye and settled firmly in her mind. The compact, precisely rounded girth of Annabel's body beneath the sky-blue blouse, the neat trim of her waist, the sway of her grey skirt when she walked her stylish walk – such things, to Pauline's surprise, gradually recalled obscure images and sensations of her early childhood at Falcon's Point, her parents' cottage in Yorkshire. But why? That had been over ten years ago, before she had reached the age of five. What connection could there be? Pauline puzzled it over, but to no avail.

Unlike many, Annabel was reasonably civil towards her. One afternoon when Pauline's pen had run out, Jamey, in her customary manner of impersonal politeness, had readily supplied her with ink. This small act produced an odd mixture of gratitude, resentment and admiration in Pauline. The cocoon of her emotions tightened even closer around her, and she found it impossible to exchange anything but the occasional few monosyllables with Annabel.

Yet the fascination remained, spiced with pungent but confused memories from the distant past, and it grew more intense as the winter approached.

During one particularly dull French lesson, last period of the day, Pauline found herself staring discreetly at her Form Captain as the latter frowned in concentration over a text-book in her lap. Annabel had pushed her chair back a little way and drawn her legs right up until the heels of her shoes, pressing down on the seat of the chair, were almost in contact with her haunches – the kind of careless posture common in the innocent world of convent schools. Pauline's eyes followed the folds of Annabel's skirt, which trailed loosely down and backwards; she noted the embroidered trimming of the white petticoat, the coarser pattern of the white cotton socks which encased the calves up to the knees; and her gaze settled on the tensed thighs, sheathed in nylon tights and exposed almost to the buttock... warmth, shadow, mystery... polished limbs... more recollections, exciting and hot, melted and stirred in the depths. Pauline strove to bring them to light. A view of the garden at Falcon's Point... running up the staircase... but nothing more. Annabel, still oblivious of Pauline's scrutiny, replaced the book on her desk and resumed her normal position, feet once more on the floor.

As an older schoolgirl, now sixteen years of age, Pauline was familiar with most of the sexual permutations which preoccupy adolescents. Am I a lesbian? she thought, anxiously crossing the gloomy quad that evening after prep. I haven't been up until now. Do I find Annabel sexually attractive? Arousing? Well, I was certainly excited by the sight of so much of her legs. I suppose it must be physical... but why, why does it carry me off to this dreamland of years ago, to a place hundreds of miles from here? Something about Annabel makes me feel so... so completely fulfilled I want to dissolve and fade away... I don't want to live anymore when I'm close to her. Do I want to touch her? Pauline dared not answer this, even to herself, but the sudden hard pounding of her pulse was sufficient reply. I must be queer after all, she concluded despondently. Best to keep well away from Annabel James. Bottle it up, hide it away – only a few more months of this place left, anyhow.

But the problem wasn't so easy to contain. Indeed, the Christmas Dance almost blew the cork noisily off the bottle.

Sister Helena, sticking bravely to her progressive principles, had for some years allowed a coach party of fifth-year girls to travel to a Christmas Dance – a discotheque plus soft drinks – at a boys' day school near Bristol. It was, needless to say, a decent, respectable public school; teachers hovered about dutifully and kept an eye on the proceedings, and nothing embarrassing or untoward had yet occurred. Sister Helena considered this annual excursion to be useful preparation for her girls' impending encounter with the harsh world outside.

At the last moment, Pauline decided to go, perhaps because she knew that Annabel was sure to be in the party. And of course, Annabel was, along with almost a hundred others. It was the most popular outing for years, and two coaches were needed on the evening.

For Pauline, it was a distressing experience. There were more girls than boys, but even if the numbers had been reversed it was most unlikely that she would have been asked to dance. She stood in a corner of the hall, one of a group of neglected ugly ducklings, and observed the garish lights and jiggling bodies with a hard bitter disdain. But at times her gaze softened – whenever, that is, she looked at Annabel dancing. Jamey was stunning this evening. Her hair was specially groomed and thickened for the occasion; she wore a tight white t-shirt that flaunted the high bulging studs on her chest, and clinging trousers of a shining pink surface that made the wild lights shimmer and scintillate over every curve as she danced. And how expertly she danced! Pauline sipped desperately at her cola and tried not to stare too much.

The slow dances came at the climax of the evening. One of the boys – the lucky one that Annabel had chosen – embraced her and the pair began to sway in leisurely rhythm to the music. There were only a few couples on the floor now, and Pauline could not avoid noticing Annabel unless she turned right away. The hand gripping her drink began to tremble as she watched the boy ease his hands down over the lustrous swellings of Annabel's backside... Pauline felt tears suddenly stab at her eyes... the hands circled deftly and started to press the smooth pink... Annabel shut her eyes and clasped her arms tighter around the boy's neck... she laid her head on his shoulder...

One of the ducklings leaned over to Pauline.

"Are you okay, Potty?"

Pauline turned, in a frenzy of tearful rage.

"Oh, piss off!"

She threw the glass to the floor, where it smashed angrily, and ran out into the corridor, leaving several startled faces behind her. Then she leaned over the ledge of an open window and wept silently into the cold night, mumbling intermittently... "The tart! The filthy tart! I'll get her, the bitch! I'll kill her!"

At length she calmed down. Fortunately the corridor was empty. No-one had come after her. The outburst in the dance-hall would be put down to frustration, depression, any one of the hundred neuroses which afflict teenage girls; probably the others had forgotten all about her by now. Pauline was, above all, angry with herself for yielding so abjectly to her feelings, which were anyway absurd. She was very seldom given to tears. But then, when she recalled Annabel's eager writhings on the dance-floor, the dazzling sheen of those pink trousers, a sob sprang sharply to Pauline's throat, and she barely succeeded in checking it. Nothing, nothing in the world could possibly be as desirable as Annabel's body. It aroused an ache deep in Pauline that was utterly primitive, far beyond the narrow borders of reason. This was more than a schoolgirl crush. Annabel was a handsome, sexy girl, but there were many others at St Margaret's just as good-looking and sexy as her. Why this mad obsession with Annabel? She could no more explain it than subdue it.

Christmas with her family in London was as arid as ever. Pauline thought several times of asking her parents about Falcon's Point, which they had sold many years earlier, but she never did: there wasn't even a proper question to put to them. She realised that she was chasing mists in a shadowy, nebulous world and would never get to the bottom of her infatuation with this girl. But since the dance a feeling of profound betrayal had remained to trouble her, a stiff knot in her heart that might never be untied. Annabel had hurt her and she was angry.

## III

WHEN THE SPRING TERM arrived Pauline changed her position in the classroom, sitting in the row ahead so as to reduce the visual and, she hoped, the emotional distraction of Annabel's presence. She began to take walks, despite the unpleasant weather. There was a gap in the railings just beyond the sports pavilion, and whenever possible she would slip away for an hour or two and stroll through the woods – always in galoshes, for the countryside was hilly and the going somewhat wet and muddy.

During one of these strolls she found herself on unusually high ground and, discovering a widening path, she pushed on until the wood opened precipitously onto a fairly narrow but deep river, surprisingly far below, rushing busily on its way to the Devon coast. The path continued over a small stone bridge supported by a tall arch, and disappeared into more woods on the other side. Pauline was enchanted by this unexpected picturesque gorge and soon came to frequent it. The bridge, though eroded and crumbling, was quite sound, and she loved to lean over the thick stone parapet and gaze at the racing, muttering water some twenty feet below. Not once did she encounter another person. Obviously the bridge was used hardly at all in the winter months, and Pauline came to regard this desolate spot as her own special territory, her haven of tranquillity. Inspired by its air of seclusion, mystery and pristine freshness, she named the place "Eden Bridge".

Life at school proceeded tolerably for a while, though Pauline still endured the occasional pang – whenever she saw Annabel direct her vivacious smile at one of the male science teachers; whenever she saw her demurely raise fork to mouth in the Dining Hall; whenever she saw her crouching gracefully in the Library for a book on the bottom shelf, little gold crucifix trembling on its slender chain as she leaned forward. At night, in her dormitory, such images of Annabel would keep her awake for many hours. The strange yearning never left her.

One drizzly afternoon, shortly before half-term, the games staff organised a special practice match between the First and Second hockey teams. The First Eleven wore the school colours – white shirt, royal blue skirt and socks – and the Second wore all black.

Quite soon the First Team had built up an impressive lead and Annabel, St Margaret's star forward, was searching for her hat-trick of goals. Pauline, at half-back, was having a wretched time.

Early in the second half, while the Second scrambled forward in a massed assault, one of the First's defenders struck a long, penetrating ball towards the sideline of the opposition half. The counter-attack was on. Pauline, rather further back than usual, ran across to intercept. Looking round, she saw Annabel racing up to contest the loose ball. Pauline knew that she would reach the ball well before her opponent but, seized by a sudden exhilarating impulse, she slowed down; poised herself; and as Annabel lunged forward, Pauline swung her stick carefully over the ball and thrashed the Captain of St Margaret's First Eleven on the inside of the calf.

Annabel gave a short, high scream of pain and astonishment. The ball rolled over the line and Pauline ran to retrieve it. By the time she had picked it up and turned, Annabel had hobbled to the edge of the pitch. Here she threw down her stick, dropped to one knee, pulled down a sock and began frantically to rub a bright red weal on her calf. The tawny eyes blazed up at Pauline as she strode past, ball in hand.

"You pig!" exclaimed Annabel. "You did that deliberately!"

Too excited to speak, Pauline ignored her and rolled the ball back into play. Then she rejoined the game, leaving Annabel to massage her stinging leg.

For the next few minutes Pauline was in an ecstasy of guilty elation, and played some inspired hockey. Annabel was nowhere to be seen. The Second Team scored a couple of goals, and the game began to surge rapidly from one end of the pitch to the other. The First hung on to its lead, however, and finished strongly, mounting a heavy attack in the closing minutes.

From the sideline, one of the First's forwards crossed the ball and it streaked dangerously in front of the Second's striking circle. Pauline intercepted, and deftly dribbled the ball to safety by the other sideline.

As she was about to pass forward, she heard the swish of wood through air close by and, at virtually the same instant, felt a terrific crack at her ankle. Nobody, thought Pauline, as the wood made resounding contact with her bone – nobody could possibly strike with *that* much power! Then there was no thought, only, it seemed, an odd gap where her left foot had been. Bereft of support, her leg collapsed and Pauline found herself sprawled on the ground. Legs and clubs whirled in and out of view, and then she was alone on the turf, clutching her ankle, bracing herself for the wave of agony which, already, she felt approaching.

Moments later the game ended. Victory for the First Team, as usual. But Pauline cared little about the score. She lay crumpled on the field, gritting her teeth, confused, weak, helpless – concentrating everything on her hand as it gripped the ankle in a vain effort to keep down the excruciating spasms of pain. Her left foot seemed entirely numb. Tears came to her eyes and went, quickly. She rolled her head in the damp grass. Dimly she was aware of the players leaving the pitch. Then, close by her face, she made out a pair of hockey shoes. Royal blue socks, drawn trimly up to the knees…

Annabel was standing over her, legs a little apart, hockey stick cocked jauntily over one shoulder.

"I don't like dirty play, Potter." The exquisite upper lip was curled in contempt. "But if you want to play the game like that, sweetie, you'd better realise I can hit pretty damn hard."

Pauline's vision, considering the pain she was in, was remarkably clear. Dumbly, she looked up along the sinuous length of the limbs that towered above her; she caught the slightest, silliest of details, such as the splotch of dried mud high on the inside of Annabel's bronzed thigh, not far below the triangle of navy-blue gym-knicker which, from Pauline's position, was easily discernible under the short hockey skirt.

Annabel seemed annoyed by Pauline's refusal – inability – to make any reply.

"You can forget about the First Team as long as *I'm* around. We can do without your sort – *Potty!*"

She snorted derisively and sauntered away, an animal splendid in conquest. Pauline, still too dazed to be angry, stared in silence at the bold, self-assured athletic stride, at the way the little pleated skirt twitched obediently over the buttocks, step after step, at the expertise with which she juggled and tossed that hardest, deadliest, sweetest of hockey sticks.

And after the long limp back to the pavilion, after the two days spent nursing the throbbing ankle, Pauline was still in rather a daze. The shock of physical injury, even if comparatively slight, will often alter one's habitual reactions. Pauline was aware that she should feel bitterly humiliated, infuriated; and part of her did indeed smart at the wound that had been inflicted. But other parts of her reacted differently. Something of the elation she had felt after hitting Annabel remained, despite the devastating retribution which had followed; and the retribution itself was, on reflection, almost as pleasurable as it was painful. She felt a particular pride in having claimed so much of Annabel's attention that afternoon – she had left her mark, physically as well as emotionally, on the marvellous girl for just a while, and that seemed to justify everything. The incident served to intensify her desire for something more: an overwhelming urge to vindicate herself completely, to make one supreme gesture of self-assertion. She knew, somehow, that Annabel had to be an intimate, almost loving participant: her involvement was essential. But why? And, perhaps more to the point: how?

Pauline did not have long to wait before both questions were answered.

# IV

THE HALF-TERM BREAK had ended. Winter eased off a little, melting into the rain and sharp March winds which periodically lashed the countryside. The wind drove in noisy gusts at Pauline one evening after Dinner as she crossed the quad of St Margaret's. She strolled past the Chapel, eerie in the darkness, and at length arrived at the Science Block, brashly white even at this hour. All was dark inside, as Pauline had expected, and the doors were locked; but she had prevailed upon Miss Davis, the Head of Science, for permission to use the Caretaker's keys and retrieve her Physics exercise book in order to complete some neglected homework. She let herself in, switched on the corridor light, and made her way silently along until she reached the Physics Lab. In a few seconds she had located her book and she duly returned to the corridor. As she passed the Biology Lab she heard a moan, low but distinct.

Pauline stopped sharply. There was no other sound in the building. All was perfect hush. She waited for what seemed a whole minute, and just as she was about to walk on she heard it again: a girl's moan, this time longer and deeper.

Hurriedly she switched off the light and fumbled in her coat pocket for her torch. She approached the door marked "Biology". She tried the handle. Locked. She took the keys from her pocket and tried a few of them until the lock turned. Holding her breath, she tip-toed in. Now the noise was loud and clear. Another moan, this time of delighted astonishment, from behind the door across the darkened lab… from the stock-room, which was sure to be locked as well. Pauline crept over to the door. This final barrier she couldn't cross without revealing her presence, which she dared not do. She placed her ear against the wood and clearly made out the sounds within: a steady rhythmic panting, sighs, gasps, frequent moans; occasionally a man murmuring; now a girl's ecstatic cries, short but alarmingly loud, accompanied by faster panting and increasingly urgent gasps.

Hastily, aware that time was running out, Pauline shone her torch around the lab. On the table nearest the stock-room door was a small pile of books; next to it lay a man's sports jacket, discarded in an untidy heap. Quickly she searched through the pockets, and found a wallet. Opening it, she pulled out a Driving Licence. On it was written "Dennis Roger Murray". Mr Murray: the new Biology teacher. Pauline's mind sprinted; perspired with visions. She turned her attention to the books: science texts, a pencil case, at the bottom a Biology exercise book. She shone the torch on this last item, and the name written there seemed, in some bizarre way, to be just the one she had expected to find, even though the sight of it made her mind reel: Annabel James.

From the stock-room a long and terrible cry, as of a woman joyfully abandoning life.

Successfully preventing herself from thinking, Pauline pocketed the Driving Licence and the exercise book. She returned the wallet to the jacket. Then, desperately congratulating herself on her presence of mind, she stole out and re-locked the Biology Lab with absolute precision and silence.

Next morning Pauline saw Matron and obtained permission to miss lessons for the day. Not much was required to convince Matron that she was ill, for Pauline looked unusually drawn and feverish.

There was only one place to go. She left the school, cut through the woods, and within twenty minutes was at Eden Bridge. Here, as was her custom, she leaned over the parapet and looked downstream at the surging water.

This morning she remained thus far longer than normal.

20

Thoughtfully she began to survey the high steep banks of the river. On one side, her right, was a considerably lower embankment of worn granite, now largely overgrown with sinister nettles and thick long grass, which followed the river for some distance before giving way to the natural steep bank of bushes and trees. Probably it had been used many years ago for mooring small pleasure boats.

Pauline turned back to the wood. Soon she found what she knew must be there, however densely overgrown: a slender pathway, descending abruptly from the main track, and studded with flat stones to form an improvised stairway. In a few seconds she was down on the embankment. Her brow furrowed as she gazed alternately at the water below and the bridge above her. She strolled along the embankment, inspecting its length and glancing occasionally across the river.

Her attention was caught by the carcass of a half-eaten bird, lying next to a thick growth of nettles. She crouched down and ran her finger over the wicked prickly leaves.

Then, very suddenly, her face broke into a smile.

A little furtively, the two girls entered the Chapel, which was dim and quite deserted. Annabel sat down at the end of a bench, Pauline stood nearby in the aisle.

"Well, Potter, what is it?"

"I advise you to keep your voice down."

Annabel coolly crossed her legs and glanced at her watch.

"We've only got fifteen minutes of Lunch Break left. And I've still got things to do. So please get on with it."

"All right, then. I'll come straight to the point." Pauline swallowed, checking that her throat was clear. "Can you tell me where your Biology exercise book is – at this very moment?"

Annabel gaped at her, eyes flashing, then quickly shut her mouth and looked away.

"Well… I'm not really sure, offhand. Why do you ask?"

"Because I found it yesterday evening. In the Biology Lab."

Annabel shut her eyes, as if about to launch into fervent prayer. She made no other move.

"And do you know what else I found there last night?"

"No." Annabel's eyes remained closed. Her voice had dropped to a murmur. "What else?"

"Most peculiar, really, but I found a gentleman's Driving Licence – right next to your book."

Annabel did not attempt to feign ignorance. Slowly she uncrossed her legs and leaned forward.

"Oh God. So it *was* taken."

"Yes. It was." Pauline marvelled at her own self-possession. But now she was an artist, inspired, conceiving her masterpiece. "And do you know what I heard from inside the stock-room? *The* most extraordinary noises!"

Annabel put elbows on knees and head between hands. She stared at the floor. Her tormentor proceeded.

"Do you know what Sister Helena would do if informed about the things I saw and heard last night?"

The head shook slowly.

"No? Well, I'll tell you." Pauline's voice rose, echoed round the melancholy walls of the Chapel. "There's only one thing she *could* do: get rid of the culprits. The vile fornicators! Get rid of them, cast them out forever! Sack him, destroy his career. Expel her, shame her family – "

Annabel tried desperately to rally.

"You can't prove a thing. Just because you stole – "

"As soon as I left the Science Block last night I went straight across to the Prefects' Common Room with your book. I asked for you and you weren't there. Not even your best friends knew where you were. Then I did the same in your dormitory. Again, none of your neighbours knew."

She paused. Annabel, offering no defence, stared at the floor again.

"All those people could verify your absence at that time yesterday. I'll bet Mr Murray's wife could do the same concerning her husband, if asked. And I'm sure Sister Helena *would* ask, very very carefully indeed."

"Please help me, God."

"Forget God. You'd better start thinking about *me*."

Annabel looked up sharply. "Well, why don't you go ahead and tell Sister? Ruin me. That's what you want, isn't it?"

"Yes. It's what I want. But not that way. Not necessarily."

"What do you mean?"

"Try, 'What do you *want?*'"

"Want? You mean... blackmail?" The eyes blinked rapidly, registering outrage and alarm.

"You seem to have got the point."

"But – how could you possibly? I mean, that's a *dreadful* thing to do!"

"Yes. *Dreadful.* Damned unsporting, isn't it?"

Annabel covered her face with one hand.

"Don't worry. I don't want money, or anything you can't give me."

"What then?"

"You'll find out when the time comes. Which must be soon, before all these aces fall out of my sleeve."

"Soon?"

"This afternoon, for example. Right after school."

"But I can't! I have a hockey match at four-thirty. It's vital I play!"

"To hell with the hockey. This should be more vital."

"If... I agree, will you give back those... those things you took?"

"Yes. I'll return them at once. And I'll never mention a thing to anybody."

There was a solemn pause.

"You can't possibly refuse my offer," said Pauline, more softly. "It's not only your future at stake. Remember that."

"But what on earth do you want with me?"

Pauline smiled, and took her time to answer.

"I'm sure you remember that hockey practice a couple of weeks ago... when you nearly broke my ankle at the end of the match."

"Only because you fouled me first. I only whacked you in retaliation. And to teach you a lesson."

"Well... you've hurt me in more ways than you'll ever realise. You've gone too far. Regard this as *your* lesson, your turn to take a whack."

Annabel's eyes widened.

"You mean you're going to hit me?"

"No. Not exactly. As I said, you'll find out in due course. The point is, do you accept my terms? Can you – and Mr Lover – afford to turn me down?"

"You're loathsome, Potter."

"Yes – or no?" snarled Pauline.

Annabel nervously pulled her skirt further down over her knees.

"All right then," came the reply at last. Pauline's heart gave a little jump. "Whatever you say. But you'll keep your side of the bargain?"

"Absolutely."

"But listen," went on Annabel. "I'll be free after school tomorrow. If I promise – for tomorrow – would that be all right?"

"Why should I trust you?"

"Because... because I'll promise, that's why. I was brought up to keep my promises."

"But not your virginity."

"That's no concern of yours!"

"It is now."

"Huh!"

"Hold your crucifix."

"What?"

"That crucifix you're wearing. Hold it in both hands."

Annabel obeyed, and piously clasped the gold crucifix that dangled over her chest.

"Promise you won't say a word about this, ever, to a single soul."

"I promise."

"Promise – swear to God – that you'll meet me at the pavilion at four tomorrow afternoon."

"I swear." Her eyes closed again. The long lashes quavered slightly.

"And promise you'll do everything I say for the hour after that."

Silence. The lovely bow of the upper lip curved in apprehension.

"Promise!" hissed Pauline.

Annabel swallowed. "I promise," she whispered. "I promise."


# V

THAT NIGHT THE RAIN poured down hard, swelling the river under Eden Bridge. But in Pauline's dream all was warm and resplendent as she sat on the embankment. Then there was Annabel, appearing magically, dressed in hockey kit. She smiled and began to dance, twisting her body with a passion that was almost violent, making skirt flutter repeatedly over gym-knickers. The dreamer tried to approach, but Annabel laughed and with a little-girlish, skipping run ascended some of the stones which led up to the bridge. She paused and sat down, legs wide apart, obscenely displaying her navy-blue crutch. She grinned. The face was Heavenly sweetness itself and irresistible. The dreamer crawled up towards her, negotiating the stones with distressing slowness. But now, as Annabel turned to proceed upwards and remain tantalisingly out of reach, they were on the staircase at Falcon's Point. Annabel reached the top nimbly and disappeared round a corner. Then the dreamer, with bewildering speed, was also at the top of the stairs. Still on hands and knees, Pauline turned and looked along the passage… there was a room at the end of it, into which she knew Annabel had run, closing the door behind her. Pauline crawled on… the passage darkened frighteningly, but a bar of light shone out from under the door. Behind it she could hear laughter, the high breathless laughter of a child delirious with pleasure. The girl inside was playing some sort of game. Yes – it was the room of games and fun, of lights and colours. But still the door was there, barring her way. She wept with anger and frustration as she listened to Annabel chuckling behind it. Why couldn't *she* go in and play as well? It was *her* room: of that she was certain. But Annabel had taken it over and wouldn't let her in. Pauline started to push and bang, harder and harder… until at last, without warning, the door gave and Pauline found herself high on a ledge, perilously close to falling into the river that swept along far, horribly far below. The bridge, which should have been there, had vanished, and now there was only that dizzy gap and the tumultuous water beckoning deep in the abyss. Helplessly, she felt herself slipping, screamed silently, and tumbled out of the life of dreams.

# VI

PAULINE ARRIVED AT THE PAVILION early, dressed in a warm heavy coat and carrying a long duffel bag on her back. She paced up and down along the path that led back to school, exceedingly nervous – as she had been all day, despite absenting herself from school once again. She could not have faced Annabel in the classroom. Perhaps she would never be able to again after today.

The seconds ticked by mercilessly. It was a chilly afternoon, bright in spite of the leaden sky.

Annabel appeared at exactly four. Pauline, inhaling long deep breaths of the sharp air to steady her nerve, watched her solemn approach along the path as the bell in Saint's Tower chimed in the background. Her Form Captain was dressed smartly in navy-blue blazer, grey jersey and skirt, white socks. Even when worried, she looked nothing less than immaculate... yes, she was beautiful. Pauline felt a sudden wave of panic, a conviction of her own inadequacy, and was assailed by an impulse to abandon the whole business at once and return to the warmth and safety of her dormitory. She clenched her teeth. No... no... this was her moment, her great chance. Now, or never in eternity...

And now Annabel was beside her.

"Well, here I am, Potter. Make the most of me while you can."

The defiant, almost taunting tone of her words inflamed Pauline, instantly restoring her resolve.

"Come this way," she muttered, and promptly led off across the wet field to the fence at the school perimeter.

"Aren't you going to tell me where we're going?" asked Annabel, pausing at the gap in the railings.

"You'll soon find out –"

"But we aren't allowed out of school." Annabel looked doubtful. "We really shouldn't, you know."

"You're obeying *my* rules now – remember?  So just follow me."

Her galoshes squelching over all obstacles, Pauline led the way. Annabel, wearing standard school shoes, had difficulty in making progress, and protested frequently as she followed through endless puddles and clumps of thick wet grass. Before long her white socks were soaked and mud-splattered.

"Potter!" she called. "I'm utterly drenched! How much more of this awful wood is there?"

Pauline turned, and grinned as she watched Annabel, with a brave show of dignity, try to flick some mud off the hem of her skirt.

"Not far now. Just over this hill and we'll be on the main path."

Annabel scowled, then struggled up after her.

Soon they were indeed on the path. Pauline set a brisk pace, and Annabel, now tight-lipped, lagged several yards behind. There was little to hear apart from the crunch of the girls' footsteps; occasionally there was the sigh of wind through the branches or the spirited chirping of birds.

Then, in the distance, the sound of running, lapping water.

The abrupt opening of the wood onto the gorge below never failed to excite Pauline, even after numerous visits. She waited on the bridge, and as Annabel slowly joined her Pauline realised that this was the first time anyone had been here with her. Eden would never be the same again.

"Lovely, isn't it?" said Pauline, leaning over the parapet. "Just look at that view.  Isn't it... Heavenly?" She pointed downstream, where the river flowed for almost a quarter of a mile before bending sharply out of sight.

"Most picturesque, I'm sure," replied Annabel, moving back a little. To Pauline, another human's voice sounded oddly discordant against the watery monotone.

For a minute or two they stood watching in silence. Obviously Annabel was in no hurry to urge her captor to proceed. She stood still, biting her lower lip anxiously.

At length Pauline turned to her, face set.

"We'd better start now, while it's still clear and bright."

"Oh. Start what?"

"Take off your clothes and hand them to me."

Annabel's face fell.

"Potter, you must be joking. Take them off *here?*"

"I've been here a score of times and never seen a soul. Not at this time of the year. Don't worry, nobody will see you. Only me. Now – undress."

For the first time, Pauline saw genuine fear on that normally most composed of faces. Annabel glanced round, frightened, uncomprehending, then looked back at Pauline. But the latter was unmoved.

"You promised. Remember – you swore!" Pauline held out a hand. "So give me your clothes, as I asked."

She had indeed sworn. Annabel touched her crucifix. Resigning herself to her fate, she proceeded to keep her promise.

Gingerly, she draped her blazer over Pauline's outstretched arm. Then, with an almost lazy upsweep of her arms, she pulled the jersey over her head; this too was passed to the other girl. Already Annabel began to shiver.

"Potter... it's awfully cold. I'll freeze to death."

"Get on with it," breathed Pauline. She stared grimly, determined not to miss a single detail of the metamorphosis.

Annabel sighed, unbuttoned the sky-blue blouse and slipped it off her shoulders. As Pauline took it, she leaned against the stone parapet to support her shaking legs: for Annabel wore a dramatic half-cup bra, stiffly white and embroidered with fine lace, which clutched and raised high the billowy spheres of her bosom. But Pauline's eye was at once distracted by the silky half-slip petticoat, uncovered as the skirt, with a zip and a tug, fell to the ground and spread in a grey pool around Annabel's ankles. A twist and a wiggle of the behind, and the petticoat was loosened; it whispered gently down the stockinged legs.

Once started on any job, Annabel was brisk, methodical, efficient. She stepped out of the jumble of grey and white material at her feet, crouched to pick up the discarded garments and coolly handed them to Pauline; though she avoided the latter's eyes.

Next, she bent over to attend to the muddy shoes and socks. The tights encasing her lower half were dark and slightly opaque at the top, but nonetheless the small white knickers beneath were clearly visible, particularly when Annabel bent and stretched the nylon hose to its utmost.

The speed at which all this was happening shocked Pauline. It was more than the senses could absorb: she was spellbound, yet somehow prompted, too, by something almost familiar… as if this were a ritual which had been observed or enacted many times before.

And now Annabel was peeling off the tights… rolling them down sturdy brown thighs, expertly down over calves and over ankles, finally off each foot, one after the other.

She straightened up. Hands moved to the strap at her back; the bra collapsed and unloaded the lavishly rounded breasts, freeing them to tremble over the chest. The nipples, firm and vivid in the cold air, gave them the appearance of monster-eyes, frightening almost, bulging and rolling insanely.

Instinctively, Annabel turned her back on Pauline for the last item. Fingers hooked under elastic and the brief cotton knickers were drawn down to expose her buttocks, which subsequently eased apart and downwards a little – they seemed somehow sullen and forlorn, peculiarly sad. She stepped out of the wisps of white fabric at her feet and slowly turned to face Pauline, entirely naked save for the slender crucifix around her neck.

The body was covered with goosepimples. Annabel folded her arms tight to try, in vain, to control the shivering.

"All right, Potter. I just hope you're enj-joying this more than me."

The abdomen was firm and smooth, undulating and deliciously curved – almost like a belly-dancer's. The patch of pubic hair – larger than Pauline had expected – was dark and thick. All there, all hers to command: supple, strong, sleek, completely unblemished. All else was nothing; would be nothing for however long she lived beyond this day. The power and the glory began and ended right here.

And Pauline stared and stared. How she wanted to touch and stroke her – how she had wanted to, for so many long and lonely years…

Annabel winced as a fresh gust of wind blew over the bridge.

"Are you just g-going to keep me standing here, for God's sake? L-Like this?"

Pauline forced her mind back to the necessary task.

"No," she said, in a curiously detached voice. "No. Give me the rest of your clothes."

Annabel did as requested, and Pauline bundled everything into her duffel-bag. The physical movement revived her.

"Right." Her breath steamed in the air. "Now get up on the parapet."

Annabel stopped shivering with remarkable abruptness.

"You heard me – get up there!"

A vacant, horrified expression on her face, Annabel clambered awkwardly onto the rough stone. Against it her flesh looked woefully tender and vulnerable.

31

"Now stand up. And face downstream."

Annabel obeyed.  She was shaking now with terror, not cold.

"What I want you to do, dear Jamey, is quite simple."

"Oh no… no." Annabel's words were barely audible.

"I want you to dive into the river and swim."

"Swim? But where? I'll be swept away!"

"Not if you make for that embankment, down there on the right. I'll be waiting there for you. So make sure you don't jump until I'm ready."

Annabel stared down in disbelief at the angrily swirling water. Pauline came closer to her, so that her face was no more than a few inches from Annabel's shivering buttocks. She could see every goose-pimple, every hair of the fine down at the base of the naked back; she felt a sublime giddiness sweep over her.

Annabel looked hysterically down over the back of her shoulder.

"Potter, please! I could be killed diving into that river!"

"Yes. You could be killed." Pauline smiled, as if in a trance. "But I don't really believe you will be – not a swimmer like you."

"But the water isn't deep enough for diving into!"

"It's deep enough for you."

"Oh God!" Annabel glanced frantically down, then back over her shoulder again. "Potter, please, please! I'll do anything you want me to – anything! Or you can do anything you want to me. But please, don't make me jump!" Her breath was now short, rapid, uncontrolled.

What a temptation it was to touch her: to feel her, to press, probe and finger her, every inch of her. To enter that room at last… there was a flowering of images and sensations as she recalled the dream.

"Potter! Are you listening, for heaven's sake?"

The high-pitched shout spoiled Pauline's reverie. She looked up, annoyed.

"Yes, I'm listening. But it won't do any good. You're going to jump, so get ready!"

With that, she moved off; leaving Annabel wide-eyed and open-mouthed, poised unsteadily on the parapet.

In moments, Pauline had descended the steps and was down by the foot of the bridge. She looked up. Annabel had improved her balance, adopting a star-fish position: her arms were outstretched sideways and her legs were spread wide. At the junction of the fore-shortened limbs was plainly exposed the thick tuft of pubic hair. At the twin points of her raised chest, stiff nipples stood out against the louring sky. The face that looked down imploringly at Pauline was distorted with torment and despair. The figure reminded her, with a divine-hellish thrill, of the crucified Saviour. Your Calvary is here, murmured the sky. God is violated yet again, and Heaven will weep for human souls.

Pauline turned and hurried several yards along the embankment.

Satan steadied her again. (It must be him; she was now convinced that he was aiding, inspiring her.) She dropped the duffel-bag and from it calmly drew her hockey stick.

"I'm ready now!" she called up.

From Annabel, another fearful glance at the water.

"Come on... jump!" shouted Pauline. "Get it over with!"

Arms quivering at either side, Annabel swayed as if to leap. But she stopped, shut her eyes and began to weep silently – her arms still outstretched. Breasts and stomach shuddered convulsively as she sobbed.

Jump, jump!" yelled Pauline. "You promised, you swore! Dive in! Now!"

Annabel's eyes widened suddenly and the crying ceased. Her hands flew to her crutch, as she lost control of her bladder and proceeded to wet herself. She looked down in horror as her pee dribbled through her fingers.

"Oh, Father!" she wailed. "Save me!"

"Jump! Jump! Jump!" Pauline ran in a wildly broken line to the end of the embankment. She was elated by the sight of Annabel's infantile disgrace.

Hands still clutched over her genitals, Annabel lifted her face mournfully to the sky. She composed herself. Her eyes closed, calmly, almost serenely, and her body relaxed; her lips seemed to move briefly; and to Pauline's astonishment she raised her arms and in one violent movement flung herself off the bridge.

Later, Pauline could never recall whether the moment of Annabel's suspension in the air was the longest or the shortest second she had ever experienced. It was like a measureless vacancy in the fabric of time and existence, an abrupt nothing where, a heartbeat earlier, there had been everything.

Then an uproar in the water, as Annabel, still horizontal, met it with an explosive crash – achieving the most grotesque of belly-flops.

Pauline was vaguely aware of a high screech from somewhere on the surface of the river, followed by a glimpse of struggling arms and Annabel's face, shockingly transfigured by water, pain, by the mouth gaping hugely, desperately for air. Limbs thrashed and were swept along, tossed helplessly over and over by the mad current.

For a moment Pauline was sure that she would drown. But Annabel was drifting closer and closer as she hurtled along, moving in an increasingly decisive diagonal towards the embankment; and it was soon clear that she had enough strength to reach the point where Pauline stood.

She held out the hockey stick. Seeing it, Annabel redoubled the vigour of her strokes and put all her might into one determined grasp at the crook of the stick, which was poised just above the water. She grabbed it with both hands and gasped with relief.

Pauline was jolted hard by the weight of the struggling body, but held fast to the handle.

Potter!" Annabel scarcely had breath enough to speak. "Pull me out!"

Pauline made no reply. She gazed, enthralled, at the mess of sleeked-back wet hair over Annabel's head, at the straining muscles of her arms, at the agitated kicking of the powerful legs, at the water foaming about the bouncing buttocks, at the dangling breasts… and at the expression of panic and helpless pleading in the face, at the gorgeous mouth, now crazily distorted and turned down at the corners as if about to bawl childishly. And the water approved of it all with a continuous devilish rush: Go on! it roared, Go on! You're almost there now! *In there!* We've opened the door for you: now go on in!

"Potter! Pur-lease! Pull me out!" Annabel urged more frantically at the stick. "I can't hold on much longer!"

Called back to half-reality by her piercing voice, Pauline, angered, shook the stick roughly. Fearing that she was about to be cast off, Annabel screamed – so loudly that even the river was inaudible for a moment.

"It's over, Jamey!" bellowed Pauline, almost laughing. "It's all over! You're done for!"

"No…!" came the cry from below. "God, no, please… pull me, please!"

"How does it feel, *sweetie?* Come on, tell me! How does it feel, just for once, to be on the receiving end? Show me!" She gave another wrench to the stick, and Annabel screamed again.

And how the water chorused!

"Come on, sweetie!" sneered Pauline. "Beg me! Beg, beg, beg!"

Annabel swallowed, fought hard to control herself, and gasped out the required sentence.

"I beg you, please… pull me out! Please!"

"Beg harder!"

Annabel hung her head and whimpered.

"I said *harder*, you bitch!"

Annabel tried again, now groaning out the words.

"I beg, beg, beg you please. I beg you, pull me out…"

"Beg me to forgive you for all the times you've hurt me! Go on! Beg for my forgiveness!"

"Forgive me… please… for all the times…"

"I beg you to forgive me *Pauline*. Go on! Say it!"

Annabel's phrases were now punctuated with sobs and barely coherent.

"Please Pauline forgive… I beg you forgive me please… Pauline… I beg you… Oh, God! Help me, help me *please*!"

Pauline leaned forward and, aiming carefully, spat in Annabel's face. The latter flinched.

"Now beg me to spit on you again, you Hell-bound whore! Come on! Again! 'Please spit on me…' "

"Beg… I beg you…"

The legs had stopped kicking now, and there was an ominous weakness in the way Annabel's body was bobbing with the water.

"Beg you… I beg you… please …. spit on me again, Pauline… Please spit on me…"

Pauline laughed and complied at once, propelling spittle in several vicious bursts all over Annabel's hair and face. This time she took it without flinching, and closed her eyes meekly.

"Now beg some more, you bitch. Beg forgiveness for all your sins! For all those pigs who've filthied your cunt! Beg, slut!"

"I can't... Ohh... *I can't...*" Annabel broke at last and began to bawl wretchedly, blindly, like a thrashed infant. The stick shook and heaved in spasms with the pressure of her sobs as she went on deliriously, whining and puling; until, at length, in exhaustion, her grip began to loosen, and her hands slipped down to the very bottom of the crook. Her feet slowly pointed downstream. She moaned feebly and eased her blubbering face into the water – preparing, it seemed, to surrender and yield herself to the river.

It was over. Pauline knew that she had won. The victory was complete, and now she could show mercy.

"All right! Hold on tight!" She pulled hard at the stick. Annabel, reviving one last time, clung on while Pauline, flexing what seemed like every muscle, dragged her, flopping, lopsided, up onto the embankment as if she were a wounded seal. Annabel moaned and twitched as her breasts and belly, then the front of her thighs, were scratched and stung by nettles; but such pains were paltry details. At last completely out of the water, she relinquished the hockey stick and collapsed, allowing tired flesh to sink in relief over stone and weeds alike. Dry land had taken her back: that was all that mattered. Now she could sleep.

Pauline relaxed and dropped the stick. She stood up straight. The sound of the river had receded strangely; the element had given up its nymph and now withdrew, turning its attention back to the sea. Evening was coming. The air was fading into dusk. Now, at last, this naked, limp body, prostrate on its belly, the spirit vanquished and fled, was here. The time had come... no, returned, after all these years.

She knelt down. Tentatively, almost timidly, she began with both hands to feel... starting with the wet hair, then the shoulders, the back, the waist... all yielded to her hands. She moved down to the thighs, softly, lovingly caressing over, along, between them. In obedience to her touch, Annabel's legs eased slowly apart, wider and wider, until all was revealed. Pauline stroked, petted the buttocks, running her finger up and down along the warm crevice between the fleshly mounds. The body remained motionless, as if dead. It was all here. No mystery was left to unveil. Time curled back upon itself and she was again goddess of all creation, as she had been many years before in that room at the end of the corridor... in the nursery at Falcon's Point when her mother had one day given her a being of breath-suspending beauty to play with. It too had been smooth, rounded, obedient to her every touch and felt delicious beyond anything else in existence. She recalled – how had she ever forgotten? – the name of that wonderful doll: Miss Perfect.

*Now look after Miss Perfect, Pauline. Be good to her*

Smooth, perfect... she recalled the olive-hued sleekness of its body beneath the dolly-clothes, beneath the blue frock and white socks, the frilly petticoat and white dolly-drawers. How she had loved repeatedly to dress and undress it, adoring the variations of its perfection! She recalled the silkiness of its dark brown hair as she ran her palm over it, nestled her little finger in the depths of it.

*Miss Perfect is very special, dear. You must treat her properly, all the time*

She had entwined herself around, within the doll until their souls had merged and melted into a sweet bliss that was the promise of God's Heavenly Kingdom to come.

And then, in the midst of this joy and reverence, the drop of Devil-poison – clouding, darkening, befouling...

*You must try hard to behave like Miss Perfect, dear*

*Try – try hard*

Spreading inky ugly blackness everywhere in her heart...

*If you're not sure how to behave properly, just think of Miss Perfect*

Until she could no longer bear the creature…

*Really! I'm sure Miss Perfect would never have done a thing like that!*

The traitor! It had finally twisted and torn her heart until it could no longer be allowed to dwell there…

*Miss Perfect is always right*

*Remember: Be Perfect!*

Ruin it! Destroy it! Before it hurts any more!

*Miss Perfect*

*Be Perfect*

*Per-fect!*

Monster, monster, you had to go!

She remembered stealing out of the house one cold morning, the doll concealed beneath her coat. She had run hastily to the river and placed Miss Perfect on the grassy bank – had let go, and watched with dumb wonder as the precious-detested Perfection had toppled and plunged with fearful speed into the water and been swept away forever… Never again would she see it, clasp it to herself. She recalled dissolving into tears at the realisation that it was lost for ever and ever (which wasn't right, wasn't the way all those stories ended). But it had been tainted, corrupted; it was no longer the beautiful pure love of the earlier time. Why did things have to change, go away?

And how could you love and hate at the same time? It was something no god could explain, or allow.

Pauline gave it all up. She returned to the girl lying before her. The spell was broken. The demon was gone, cast out. The way ahead was straight and true and calm.

Pauline rose to her feet, and from her duffel-bag drew a large towel. She covered Annabel's shoulders with it and began to rub gently. There was a sobbing sniff, the last small tremor of the eruption.

"It's all right, Jamey. Come on, sit up. You must dry yourself now."

Annabel moaned and stirred. Pauline grasped her carefully beneath the shoulders and lifted. There was a responsive movement of the legs and the girl finally managed to twist herself into a sitting position. Pauline was surprised to see that the front of the body was mottled with red and white blotches, and lightly scratched in places. The crucifix was gone, torn away and devoured by the river.

"Will you be all right?"

Annabel looked away from her and nodded.

"Here… dry yourself, quickly, and put your clothes on."

Pauline pulled the garments from her bag and placed them as tidily as she could on the ground. Falteringly, Annabel attempted to dry herself with the towel. She was still a little dazed.

"And I haven't forgotten these, either."

Pauline drew an exercise book from her pocket and handed it over. It took a moment or two for Annabel to grasp the significance of this. Then she glanced up sharply.

"Don't worry, his Licence is in the book. You see, I keep my promises too."

Annabel turned away again, and began to wipe herself a little more effectively. Pauline watched her for a while, until at length Jamey dropped the towel and awkwardly draped her blazer over her shoulders.

Pauline reclaimed the towel and picked up her bag.

"I'm going now. You can find your own way back to school."

"Yes."

She began to walk lightly towards the bridge, but after a few paces stopped and turned.

"There's one last thing."

Annabel, hunched in her blazer, looked round.

"What?"

"Remember, remember…" Inscrutably, Pauline smiled at her: "Just… be Perfect!"

*Book Two*

# PAST PERFECT

Timeframe: 1999

The deeps have music soft and low
When winds awake the airy spry,
It lures me, lures me on to go
And see the land where corals lie.

Thy lips are like a sunset glow,
Thy smile is like a morning sky,
Yet leave me, leave me, let me go
And see the land where corals lie.

*Richard Garnett*


Without the shedding of blood
there is no forgiveness

*Hebrews 9:22*

# I

## REUNION

IT WAS MIDSUMMER EVE. As the unclouded sun sank behind the Great Hall of St Margaret the Martyr School, it cast long brooding shadows over the car park in front of the red-bricked Victorian building. At exactly eight o'clock this particular year – the hundred and fifteenth anniversary of the School's foundation – a gleaming silver sports coupé pulled into the car park and crunched the gravel surface as it stopped to join the row of vehicles already parked there. From the passenger seat emerged Annabel James, wearing a dark blue cocktail dress with thin shoulder straps and a low-cut neckline that boldly showed off her cleavage. She was quickly followed by her partner Philip, dapper and self-assured in grey evening wear.

Philip put his arm around her bare shoulder as they made their way to the Great Hall. She walked carefully over the gravel in her stiletto shoes.

"How many of these Annual Reunions have you been to?" he asked. "Twenty? I think you said you hadn't missed one since you left the School."

"Nineteen," replied Annabel with a smile. "I missed one about ten years ago."

"Admirable loyalty. They must like you here."

"And I like them. Some of my happiest memories are of this place. Five of my best years."

"I guess you were a very successful pupil."

"Yes, on the whole – apart from the odd hiccup." She straightened her collar necklace.

They strolled through the imposing entrance porch and soon arrived in the Great Hall, wood panelled and ornately decorated in classic Victorian style. The ceiling was high above their heads, allowing upper floor galleries to run on all four sides. The spacious Hall was laid out with "Happy Reunion" banners and long tables bearing food and drink. Groups of women in party dress, St Margaret's alumnae of widely varying ages, milled around happily as jazz music played discreetly in the background. As was customary, a number of former teachers, all women, had turned up to join in the festivities. Here and there a few men hovered about, a little awkwardly, conscious that this event was being held for the enjoyment of their female partners. As they moved up to one of the tables, Philip looked round.

"Uh-oh. Looks like your fan club approaching fast…"

Four thirty-something ladies swept towards them: Trudi, Penny, Jo and Mizzi, some of the chief members of Annabel's gang during her St Margaret's career.

"Annabel!" called Trudi.

"*Doctor* James!" cried Penny.

Both ran into Annabel's arms simultaneously and hugged her adoringly. The other two quickly reached Annabel and each kissed one of her cheeks from the side. Impressed by this intense huddle of female amity, Philip smiled and stepped back.

"Oh Annabel, it's been *much* too long!" said Trudi, gently smacking her old friend's bottom.

"I know," apologised Annabel, briefly kissing Trudi's lips. "A whole year already!"

"I miss you so much. And the old days…" said Mizzi, affectionately touching Annabel's dark brown hair with her finger. "Ooh – those curls really suit you."

"I'm sorry I've been out of touch – but I'm just *so* busy all the time," said Annabel, also kissing Mizzi. "I feel bad not seeing any of you since the last Reunion. My father always told me that the older you get, the faster time runs by, and he was so right."

"But you haven't changed at all since last year, or the five years before that!" exclaimed Penny. "How *do* you keep yourself so young and trim? Oh do tell me the secret – I want to stay looking twenty-nine forever!"

"Maybe having a handsome new boyfriend every year?" interjected Trudi, looking pointedly round at Philip, who had begun a conversation with Jo.

"It certainly helps," smiled Annabel. "At any rate, I can tell you it's better than being married. It's much sexier when you don't have to live with your man all the time."

"How long were you with Andrew?" asked Penny. "Five years?"

"Six," replied Annabel. "And at least one of them was happy! But we were both too obsessed with our careers. And the fact we were both in the same line of work, both working at the same hospital – that ended up making things even more difficult."

Trudi raised her eyebrows and gave Annabel a sly look.

"Any chance, you think, with this one… of having the joyful result you've always wanted?

Annabel looked round. Philip was still talking to Jo and safely out of earshot.

"No luck so far," she replied, lowering her voice. "But not through lack of trying, I can promise you."

"Oh Lord," whispered Mizzi, with a glance at Philip. "If I had him to myself I'd be trying every night! Usually I don't go for blue-eyed fair-haired men but in *his* case…"

"Oh you bad girl!" said Trudi. She handed Annabel a glass of punch.

"He's rather yummy," said Penny. "Reminds me of a young Robert Redford."

"Is he… passionate?" asked Mizzi.

"*Very* passionate!" replied Annabel, keeping her voice down. "I haven't been so thoroughly serviced since university days. Some nights he doesn't let me sleep at all."

"Oh you *poor* thing! I feel *so* sorry for you!" groaned Trudi.

"But no sign of any result yet?" asked Mizzi.

"No, nothing. And he has two children from his former marriage, so I know he isn't firing blanks. He says he's happy to have babies with me and we're both doing everything we can to make it happen."

"Can he afford another child, with another woman?" asked Penny.

"Yes – is he well-off?" asked Trudi.

"Very," replied Annabel. "He's a lawyer with a big American pharmaceutical company. But I don't want him for his money. I have enough of my own."

"You want him for his… *passion*," declared Mizzi. "But is that enough to make you hitch up with him long-term?"

Annabel shrugged.

"In all honesty, I don't know. I wonder if I *do* know what I want anymore – emotionally, deep down inside. Maybe I'm just hard to please…"

"Maybe you need more than one lover at a time," said Penny, slanting her head archly.

The others were scandalised, though humorously, as they knew all about Penny's penchant for extra-marital adventures.

"No, I don't," laughed Annabel. "I had enough of those games when I was a student. What matters now, more than anything, is the *quality* of the passion, not the quantity."

"I agree," said Trudi emphatically. "St Margaret's girls deserve only the very best!"

All the girls concurred heartily with this sentiment, raising their glasses to the Old School. At that moment they were hailed by someone advancing across the Hall – Valerie, another one of the gang. She grabbed Jo and took her away from Philip before reaching the group.

"Thank goodness you took me away," said Jo, "before I started pawing him!"

"Oh Annabel, so good to see you!" said Valerie, kissing her cheek. "But listen, all of you, something interesting to tell you, before you see her for yourselves. You'll *never* guess who's just turned up! First time ever!"

"No, we'll never guess, so you'd better tell us," said Trudi.

Valerie took a deep breath.

"Do you remember that crazy Pauline Potter? The loony loner who hated us all the way through her five angry years at the School? A right twisted-up lesbian, as I recall."

"Oh God, yes," groaned Penny.

"I remember her, all too well," said Mizzi. "What an obnoxious bitch she was! Don't tell me she's honouring us with her presence tonight!"

Valerie nodded heavily, eyes wide in mock-horror.

Annabel's breath stopped. At once she felt chill deathly fingers closing around her chest, which began to break out into little beads of perspiration. She swallowed hard and said nothing. She looked over at Philip, but he had gone to another table to find a glass of wine.

"You remember her, don't you Annabel?" said Trudi. "We used to call her 'Potty' as I recall."

"Yes, I do remember her," murmured Annabel, forcing herself to stay calm.

"Didn't you once have a run-in with her on the hockey pitch?" laughed Jo.

"Yes, I believe so," replied Annabel, with an awkward smile. "But it was a long time ago."

"Why on earth has she come along tonight, after ignoring us all for twenty years?" said Penny.

"Come along isn't the word!" said Valerie. "You should see how she looks! Amazing! And see the cheap little tart she's brought with her! She can't be more than sixteen years old!"

"Oh Lord!" said Mizzi. "I can't wait! Where are they?"

"In the entrance lobby," replied Valerie. "Just about to come into the Hall, I would think."

"Excuse me, girls," said Annabel. "I need to see Philip about something."

She walked towards Philip in a daze, almost floating on the jaunty jazz music, which now sounded as if it were laughing at her. After all this time… after she had slowly and painfully succeeded in pushing what had happened on that cold brutal day into the deepest recess of her memory… now suddenly, without warning, the architect of her most abject humiliation was back. For what reason? She knew instinctively that Pauline had returned for *her*, for a second bite at her prey. There could be no other reason. She felt her bowels churning and sinking. Sweat clung to her ribs and her belly under the tight dress. Even her high-heeled shoes felt clammy. Finally she reached Philip.

"Bella, my love, how are you?" he smiled. "I'm glad you've managed to tear yourself away from your fan club. You look a bit over-heated. Feel like a glass of white wine?"

"Oh God yes, I do need a glass. Thanks Phil."

Annabel gulped down the wine and immediately felt a wave of

relief surge through her. She took a long deep breath. Now she was ready. What could Pauline do anyway, after all this time? She had apparently kept her promise never to tell anyone what had happened on the bridge, and if she did say anything now nobody would be inclined to believe her after so many years. Maybe she had come back for some other purpose, something entirely innocent. Yet despite all this reasoning, Annabel felt a little worm of anxiety gnawing away inside her. She had always refused to admit to herself that her humbling at Pauline's hands had left a permanent wound in her psyche, but her instinctive reaction at this very moment was demonstrating all too clearly that it had indeed done so. Fortunately she had always been adept at hiding her feelings and preserving a calm exterior.

Philip looked round and suddenly chortled.

"Good heavens, will you take a look at *those* two creatures!"

The sight that greeted them, from some fifteen metres away, was so extraordinary that Annabel immediately forgot her own anxieties. In fact she wondered for a few moments whether she was looking at Pauline Potter at all. The unkempt sandy hair had been transformed into a huge mane of bright vivid copper, falling like a cascade of flames down her back, almost to the waist; the tense acne-scarred face had been replaced by a poised, haughty countenance, painted with garish make-up that would have befitted a glam-rock celebrity at a gala night; and the broad confident smile showed off large bright capped teeth. She wore a green spangled gown that flowed down all the way to her feet and was cut on one side to expose a long thin white-skinned leg. In high heels, she was well over six feet tall and towered over – and looked down on – everyone around her. The effect was that of an exotic predatory bird parading itself in full plumage.

At Pauline's side stood her – friend? assistant? lover? – who looked like a rebellious teenager on her way to a vulgar fancy-dress party.

She wore a semi-transparent white blouse that came close to revealing her nipples on either side of an oversized stripy tie, and a tiny pleated red-check tartan skirt that only just covered her bottom. The kitsch schoolgirl outfit was completed by long white socks that reached some four inches above her knees – still far below the hem of the skirt – and a pair of white gym-shoes. Her figure was slender but shapely. She was somewhat less than medium height and stood well below Pauline, to whom she was clearly and happily subservient. For added and rather absurd effect, she carried a hockey stick and conspicuously munched chewing gum. Annabel noted that the schoolgirl had similar hair to herself – dark brown, parted in the centre, though somewhat longer than her own – and a face that looked strikingly like hers, with a straight nose, full-lipped mouth and finely shaped cheeks and chin. She couldn't help but be taken by her demeanour, which suggested fragility and childish awkwardness behind the audacious costume. She looked way out of her depth. This touched something in Annabel and made her feel sorry for the youngster. It was obvious that Pauline was exploiting her, showing her off to create a stir and cock a snook at her old School.

The entire gang strode over to Annabel and Philip, trying not to show how shocked and excited they were by the latest arrivals.

"Annabel, *can* you believe what we're seeing?" exclaimed Mizzi. "Outrageous!"

Almost breathless, Penny added a further shocking detail.

"I've just heard from Anne-Marie, Valerie's sister, that the schoolgirl isn't wearing any underwear whatsoever! She just saw her crouch down to pick up her hockey stick after dropping it, and she's stark naked under that tartan skirt! And she's completely shaved down there – smooth as a baby! Can you believe such lewdness?"

"What!" exclaimed Trudi. "No knickers? And no pubic hair? What a total slut!"

"I wondered where the smell of fish was coming from!" laughed Mizzi.

Annabel shook her head. "I'll bet the girl has been put up to it by Pauline. *She's* the one responsible for everything you're looking at. I *know* she is…"

At this point the schoolgirl turned and looked directly at Annabel for several moments, as if deliberately seeking her out. Annabel stared back, intrigued by the girl's effrontery. Then Pauline muttered something and they both moved off to a table to get drinks.

"Note that Madam Pauline hasn't looked over at us for one second," said Valerie. "She *must* have recognised one or two of us, even after twenty years!"

"She doesn't look at you – *you* look at her. That's the kind of ego-trip she's on," said Trudi.

"But she does look interesting," said Philip. "Does anyone know anything about her?"

Valerie replied tentatively.

"Well, I've just been speaking to Debbie Humphreys, who's a London journalist, and she says that Pauline *Barrie* – not Potter – is now a successful and well-known artist working mainly in the East End. She's really in with the Brit-Art crowd over there and lives that trendy hedonistic life-style to the full. She's also rumoured to be a witch or a sorcerer or something weird like that."

"Maybe she's put a spell on that little slut!" scoffed Penny.

"Is she old enough to be away from school?" asked Jo.

"I expect she goes to the kind of school where they're happy if you *don't* attend," said Mizzi.

"Probably been expelled from every school she was ever at," said Trudi with a snort.

"Should we try to talk to them?" asked Penny.

"Yes, we should," said Annabel. "They've come a long way to be here and we ought to show them a bit of courtesy and charity – you know, those Christian values that St Margaret's is supposed to represent."

There was a moment's silence as everyone focused their attention on the jazz music and the noisy hubbub of the party. Penny sighed.

"All right then. Who's going to volunteer?"

But before anyone could volunteer, they were approached by two figures who compelled immediate attention and respect: Miss Davies, the Head of Science, and Sister Helena herself, tall and grey and commanding in the way that all good Headmistresses should be. There was a chorus of affectionate welcomes and hugs, and some polite respectful conversation all round. Annabel hoped that Sister Helena hadn't noticed the two recent arrivals, but if she was aware of them she was too calm, controlled and diplomatic to make any reaction.

In due course Helena turned her attention exclusively to Annabel, who was rumoured to be one of her all-time favourite pupils. She put an arm around her shoulder and led the two of them away from the rest of the girls. Her voice was as gently authoritative as ever, but it seemed tinged with a melancholy tone that matched her long heavy black gown. She fingered the large gold crucifix on her chest. Her blue eyes looked slightly filmy.

"My dearest Annabel – how are you keeping? I'm so sad not to have heard from you since last year's Reunion. Any change in your circumstances? I see you have a most handsome man on your arm this time."

"Thank you, Sister. No, apart from the handsome man, no change. I'm so sorry I've been out of touch."

"I understand – your line of work keeps you insanely busy. I'm actually grateful to see you turn up so regularly to these events. Are you keeping healthy? Is all going well for you?"

"Yes, thank you, Sister. Everything's going well as far as I'm concerned. How are things at St Margaret's?"

"The School is doing fine, I'm pleased to say. But when I come to retire, which won't be too long from now, I will have to leave St Margaret's unfulfilled. It was always my dream to have you here as one of my teachers. You don't know how happy that would have made me!"

Annabel had had to respond to this overture several times before.

"I'm so flattered, Sister, and I know that teaching here would be a wonderful and rewarding thing to do. But at the moment I still feel I have to spread my wings and find out more about the big wide world out there. I really do miss the old School. One day, I promise you, I *will* teach here and make you proud to have me as one of your staff."

Helena smiled wistfully and her face wrinkled.

"Alas, my dear, I'm afraid it'll be too late for me."

"Why?"

Helena sighed.

"At the moment this is confidential, you understand – I know I can trust your discretion – but it looks as if retirement will be forced upon me somewhat sooner than I had expected. A month ago I received a diagnosis from my doctor which means I will probably have no more than a year left on this earth."

Annabel gasped. Instantly she felt tears pricking at her eyes.

"Oh no! What dreadful news! Oh Helena, I don't know what to say. I'm so very sorry!"

She turned and hugged Helena, who responded in kind. Suddenly she felt as if she were about to lose another parent. And she realised this might be the last time she would ever see her grand old Headmistress. She sobbed as she pressed her head against Helena's neck. Now she would never be able to return to St Margaret's as a teacher.

It was inconceivable to be here without its long-standing leader. For her, Helena *was* St Margaret's.

"Oh Annabel – my darling Annabel. You mustn't attract too much attention to us."

Annabel drew back. Helena, smiling gently, dabbed away her pupil's tears with her finger.

"I'll come to visit you!" said Annabel vehemently. "For as long as you're at St Margaret's. For as long as you're on this earth. That's a promise!"

"Then God has indeed blessed me. Nothing would make me happier than to spend my remaining time with my most treasured St Margaret's girls. And you, Annabel, are one of my most precious jewels! Now – let's rejoin the others, or they will start to think that something odd is going on!" She put her arm around Annabel's waist and they slowly walked back.

As they returned to the refreshment table, only Philip remained, loyally waiting for her. Sister Helena spoke to him briefly, smiled, shook hands, and departed.

"Where are the others?" asked Annabel, trying to conceal her distress.

Philip gestured towards the central area of the Hall, where a number of ladies and some of their male partners had begun to dance. The volume of the music had been turned up to get the dancing going and the lights had been dimmed slightly.

"Do you want to dance?" he asked.

Annabel shook her head.

"Normally I'd love to, but I'm really not in the mood right now. What I do want at the moment is another glass of wine."

Philip refilled her glass.

"Everything OK?"

"Yes – just some sad news about the teaching staff. I'll tell you about it later on. Why don't you go onto the floor and dance with one or two of the girls? I'll join you a bit later."

Philip nodded, seeing that she wished to be alone, and kissed her briefly before walking towards Mizzi and Trudi and the other gyrating bodies.

For the second time, Annabel was grateful for the relief brought by a quick intake of alcohol. As she looked pensively at the dance floor, she heard a high girlish voice at her side.

"Excuse me. Are you Annabel?"

It was the teenage schoolgirl, the object of the gang's earlier derision. Seeing her young pretty face at close range, Annabel's spirits lifted and she smiled back warmly.

"Yes, I am. Who are you?"

The girl proffered her hand.

"My name is Dolly. I'm Pauline's friend."

Annabel shook the hand, which was pale and slender and child-like, with lurid nail varnish. She looked down at the tartan skirt and recalled that the girl was naked underneath.

"Nice to meet you, Dolly. Are you enjoying the party?"

"Not much. Nobody seems to want to talk to me."

"Oh, I'm sorry. I'm happy to talk to you, if you want."

"You're very kind. I knew you would be, as soon as I saw you. And I wanted to talk to you."

"Why?"

"Well, partly because you look so charming… and partly because Pauline asked me to give you this…"

Up to now, she had concealed her hockey stick behind her back. Gingerly she brought it into view and handed it to Annabel.

"It's her old St Margaret's hockey stick. She asked me to give it to you as a peace offering. She said you'd know what it was all about."

Annabel's chest tightened and once again she felt the anxiety worm start to wriggle inside her, though now it was blunted by the wine. She examined the battered old stick and recognised it at once – it was the very same one that Pauline had used to fish her out of the river twenty years ago. She looked up at Dolly, who seemed unaware of its significance and was smiling sweetly at her.

"Did you say a peace offering?"

"That's right. She told me that she'd wronged you many years ago, and she was ashamed of what she'd done and wanted you to forgive her. Does that make sense?"

Annabel felt relieved.

"Yes, it does make sense. Tell Pauline I accept her offering and will try to forgive her. But it might take some time."

"She also asked me to give you this…"

Dolly carefully pulled a card from under the elasticated top of one of her long white socks and handed it to Annabel, who read it.

"The Black Sun Gallery… Spitalfields, London."

"That's where she exhibits her work. She'd very much like to meet you there while her current exhibition is on, if you can find any time. Do you live in London?"

"Yes, I do. In Earls Court." Annabel paused to consider the invitation before continuing.

"Tell Pauline I'll do my best, but I'm very busy a lot of the time. I work in a hospital."

"Are you a doctor?"

"Yes. Well, I'm a consultant, but it means more or less the same thing."

"I knew you'd be doing something important with your life. I wish I could."

Annabel smiled encouragingly at her.

"I'm sure you will, Dolly. What do you do at the moment? I assume you've left school?"

Dolly grinned mischievously. Her lips were painted bright scarlet. Annabel noted the light sprinkling of freckles over the bridge of her nose and her cheeks. There was a tiny gold stud on her left nostril and she wore big red plastic ear-rings.

"I like to wind people up by telling them I'm sixteen, so they think I should be at school," said Dolly. "Actually I've just turned eighteen, but I look a bit young and immature for my age. I suppose I am immature."

"I don't think you are at all. Have you left home already?"

"I've never had a home, apart from the horrible shitty places I've been sent to for as long as I can remember."

"Don't you have any parents?"

"I've never had any parents."

"Oh – I'm sorry to hear that. Where do you live then?"

"I live with Paulie – sorry, Pauline. I help her with whatever artwork she's doing. And I do whatever else she tells me to do. I'm her personal assistant."

"Does she look after you well?"

"Yes – she certainly does look after me!" This was accompanied by a short laugh.

Annabel looked pointedly at her.

"Are you happy being with her?"

Dolly nodded.

"Oh yes. It's the most interesting thing I've ever done in my life. Paulie isn't boring or stuffy. She's quite far out, you know."

"Yes. I imagine she would be. She certainly looks stunning tonight."

"I'll tell her you said so. She'll be pleased. She always speaks well of you. I've really been looking forward to meeting you."

"I hope you're not disappointed."

"No, I'm not disappointed at all. You're the most beautiful person here tonight."

Annabel caught her breath. She looked hard into the girl's green eyes.

"My goodness, Dolly, you're very direct."

"I feel like being direct when I look at you."

Annabel was taken aback by this blatant pass, but in some school-girlish way also pleased by it. She decided to return the compliment.

"Actually, you're mistaken. *You're* the most beautiful person here tonight."

Dolly looked at her with an expression bordering on ecstasy.

"Oh Annabel, you're so lovely. I'm so glad I met you! I hope I'll see you again!"

She touched Annabel's bare arm, leaned forward and slowly, lingeringly kissed her cheek, leaving behind a heavy scent of musky perfume. Then she turned and walked away.

Annabel drank what was left of the wine and leaned back against the table. As she gazed at Dolly's departing figure she felt her heart racing – this time not from anxiety. She inserted the gallery card Dolly had given her under the tight wing of her bra, beneath the dress under her arm, and was surprised to find how much she was sweating. It was a hot evening, a hot crowded party, and she was having to cope with one unexpected emotion after another. She gripped the hockey stick and wondered about Pauline. It was obvious that she had changed considerably since her school days. But could anyone change her true nature that much? Annabel's optimistic and charitable view of people required her to accept that such a transformation *was* possible, and that Pauline's peace offering was genuine. Perhaps she would take a look at her exhibition in Spitalfields. And perhaps she'd see Dolly again… the little go-between. She looked over at the girl, who had rejoined Pauline and was talking animatedly with her and one or two other people. Yes, maybe it was time to heal the old wounds.

There was a pause in the music and Philip came back to her. He had now discarded his jacket.

"Hello, Stranger. Was that the St Trinian's girl I just saw you talking to?"

"Yes, it was. She really is a sweetie. She's had a tough childhood, and I think she's going to have a difficult future. She's never had any kind of proper upbringing or guidance. Makes me realise how fortunate I've been – how fortunate all of us have been."

"Yes, I suppose so. Is that a hockey stick you have there?"

"Yes, a souvenir from the old schooldays. One day I may tell you all about it."

Philip put his arm around her.

"One day you'll tell me about a lot of things – my lovely mysterious woman."

They kissed, briefly but intensely.

"Phil – I'm feeling a bit tired all of a sudden. And I need a good long shower. Can we make our apologies and return to the hotel? I'm sorry to be such a drag."

"Not at all. I'm happy to go back. I'll speak to the other girls."

As Philip went off, Annabel walked to the large high window near to their table. The curtains were still open, to let in the last of the summer light. The sun had just set over the horizon, leaving behind it a fabulous shining lemon sky. As she looked out across the playing field, Annabel saw the big new pavilion, and next to it the new perimeter fence, now preventing any easy access to the darkening woods beyond. Over the brow of the hill, just where the sun had set, lay the gorge and the river and the old bridge. Was the bridge still there? She was suddenly seized by an urge to see it again. Could she bear to revisit the scene of her ignominious defeat? Maybe it was time to exorcise the whole thing, now that Pauline had made a friendly approach. Time to heal and time to forgive. It was what Sister Helena would want her to do.

Philip came up behind her.

"The girls are ready to say goodbye. They're disappointed you have to leave so early, but they understand..."

"Phil, can we pay a visit to the other side of those woods tomorrow morning? The weather's lovely and we have the morning free, don't we?"

"Sure we can, but it means delaying our trip to the coast."

"I'm not bothered about that. It would mean a lot to me to go and look at something out there in the woods. An old memory."

Philip was intrigued.

"Yes, of course. Whatever you want, my love."

An hour later they were back in their hotel room, a few miles from the School. Annabel walked directly to the large bed and put her necklace and watch on the side table. She kicked off her stiletto shoes and unzipped her dress, which fell to the carpet around her feet. Then she unhooked her black strapless bra, tossed it to the floor, and finally yanked down the matching lacy knickers. She turned to face Philip. Her naked body glistened with sweat.

"Phil – I'm hot and sticky and emotional. I've been on a roller-coaster tonight and the worry-worm is back in my belly. I need you to get rid of it."

Philip had encountered the worry-worm before and hastily began to undress, throwing his clothes over a nearby armchair.

Annabel sat on the plush bed, her feet on the quilt, and watched him remove his clothes with a look of breathless anticipation on her face. Sex was an addiction she would never be able to conquer. In fact she had reached the point where she loved being conquered by it. Above all she loved the pleasure of giving herself to her partners, and seeing the pleasure *they* derived from her passionate submission. Now a mature and experienced woman in her mid-thirties, she had come to accept this passive part of herself as an emotional compensation for her otherwise robust and assertive personality. Indeed she was beginning to realise that this yearning for surrender to a stronger force or a higher power had always been the most essential element of her character, which went even beyond sexual pleasure. It was a secret she had confided to only one person, her old and trusted female lover in Oxford, the only same-sex partner she had ever had; but she hadn't dared to disclose it to any of her male lovers, because she felt that her survival in the real world would be compromised by doing so. Yet increasingly she longed to share this deepest part of herself with someone, so as to be able to give herself to that person completely. She felt that one day this would happen – when she found the right partner.

Philip climbed onto the bed and she lay back on the pillows, opening her legs wide, knees sharply bent. She ran her finger up and down her moist genitals and looked at him intently.

"Are you ready, Bella?" he breathed. He was fully erect.

"Oh God yes, I've been ready for ages. I need that big beautiful thing inside me right now. Come and drill this worry-worm out of me."

As he moved closer, Annabel drew her legs up and back until her knees were at her shoulders. Then she reached down with both hands and opened herself wide. She felt she was behaving like an animal on heat but couldn't help herself. Philip entered her at once and she groaned loudly, with almost desperate satisfaction. She loved the sensation of being cleaved apart by his hardness, being opened inside again and again… and she loved the feel of his long hard body, and the hot sweaty smell of her own arousal… Their excitement mounted and they started panting, harder and faster. Her flesh rippled under the impact of his thrusts. She opened her thighs wider still, folded her knees even tighter and pressed her feet down on his lunging back, heightening her pleasure. Her groans grew longer and louder, and she forgot where she was, not caring who might overhear her lustful abandon. As Philip pumped into her with increasing urgency, making the bed creak and rock unrelentingly, Annabel's mind was filled with a kaleidoscope of images and recollections: her Biology teacher, Mr Murray, who had taken her so shamefully in the stock-room, where the cramped space had compelled her to bring her knees up almost to her head; Pauline's hands running all over her back and her thighs and her buttocks as she lay broken and beaten on the cold granite embankment; Dolly naked under the tiny tartan skirt, touching her with that delicate hand and so sweetly kissing her… To her surprise, and to Philip's, she started to come early, pushing her athletic hips faster and faster and squeezing his cock harder and harder with the contractions of her vagina. She cried out noisily, several times, as her eyes rolled up into her head and her mouth froze into an ecstatic gape. As she reached her climax and joyfully surrendered herself, twisting and jerking into one spasm after another with wild gasps, Philip accelerated his thrusts and ejaculated, flooding her with warm semen that splashed over the worry-worm again and again before at last sweeping it away.

Dolly leaned over the glass cocktail table and snorted the last of the cocaine before kneeling up sharply. She sniffed long and hard to absorb all the white powder. The hotel room undulated strangely for a few moments before returning to normal. Tonight the coke seemed to gallop inside her head with a special intensity. She remained kneeling on the carpet, since she wasn't permitted the comfort of a seat.

To her side sat Pauline, reclining in a thick armchair, still wearing her long green party gown. She caressed a slim wooden cane in her lap and gazed at Dolly with a thin-lipped smile.

"Good stuff?"

"Oh yes," sighed Dolly. "Top-grade!"

"Are you ready then?"

Dolly swallowed hard and nodded.

"All right," said Pauline. "Stand to attention!"

Dolly took a deep breath and stood up, adjusting the tartan skirt so that she looked neat and tidy. Then she walked over to where Pauline was sitting and stood smartly to attention, pushing back her shoulders and pressing her nipples against the flimsy white blouse as far as she could. She looked into the distance. Looking at the Mistress wasn't allowed without permission.

Pauline rose and stood slightly to the side of Dolly, towering over her, and looked down into her face with contempt. She grabbed the girl's hair and pulled her head back.

"You were pathetic at the Reunion tonight, you little tart. Everyone was laughing at you. I was so embarrassed!"

"I'm sorry, Paulie. I did my best for you."

"Your best is never good enough, you hopeless toe-rag. You always let me down, wherever I take you."

"Please don't give up on me. I promise to try harder."

Pauline grabbed more of the dark hair and dragged her head further back.

"Ow!"

"There's only one way to deal with you, isn't there?"

"Yes. Only one way. Ow!"

"Get up onto that armchair. Usual position."

Dolly obeyed and slowly knelt into the armchair, her chest and shoulders against the head-rest. She spread her legs wide and presented her backside to Pauline. The tartan skirt was so short that Pauline had to flip it over only a few inches to expose the entirety of Dolly's buttocks. She held the cane in her other hand.

"Lower your back and stick your arse out further, you shaven slut. Stick it right out at me!"

Dolly obeyed. Her face was now far down in the back of the arm-chair, her knees precariously at the front edge of the seat. Pauline tapped her bottom with the cane, as if testing its range.

"Stick it out further!" she snapped. "I want to see that wicked little arsehole!"

Dolly pushed out her backside to the very utmost and lowered herself still further until she showed Pauline absolutely everything she had. Her head was now almost down to the back of the seat cushion.

"Very well. Now you're going to get your just deserts, you slut!"

Dolly slowly exhaled and waited...

The Mistress always made her wait for the first one...

To build up the tension...

The cane whistled through the air and struck Dolly's left buttock with a loud whippy lash that echoed around the room. The impact shook her all the way down to her knees and her bottom instantly burned, as if seared with acid.

"Ah! Fuck!" Dolly took a sharp intake of breath. She shut her eyes tightly.

The second followed in short order, and was even harder. The stick drove the right cheek upwards for a moment before it fell back.

"Ooh! Jeez*uss!*" Instinctively she raised her body to absorb the pain.

"See what you get for being such a useless little bitch? Now come on – lower that back as I told you to, and stick your arse out properly. Can't you do anything right?"

Exhaling heavily, Dolly returned her body to the required position. Two angry red welts were now emblazoned across her backside.

The third stroke caught both cheeks at once, with a big heavy crack.

"Ohhh!" Dolly trembled as the pain coursed through her like a wave of fire. It was terrible...

A fourth stroke, at the lowest part of the buttocks.

"Ahaa... ooh!" Dolly started to jerk uncontrollably and her shoulders heaved. Then came the first sob, and a hot tear dropped onto the seat cushion. She was breaking already...

Two more strokes followed in quick succession, the second catching the outer edge of Dolly's right buttock with particular venom.

"Ooh! Shit-shit-shit! That fucking hurt!"

"Don't you swear in my company!" shouted Pauline, lashing another stroke across both cheeks. Dolly yelled again and began to cry in earnest as the last of her resistance melted away. Now she remembered that she was nobody... just an empty nothing... as always...

"My God, you're so feeble!" sneered Pauline. She pushed Dolly's body down again. The girl had lost control of herself and was twitching and shaking all over. Pauline administered two more strokes in quick succession, drawing out two more loud yells, and then saw that Dolly had taken all the punishment she could bear for this evening. Her body had crumpled into the armchair and was shuddering under the pressure of her sobs. Her backside was criss-crossed all over with vivid red stripes.

Pauline leaned over to grab her by the hair and pulled her up until their faces met. Dolly's eyes were awash; tears coursed freely down both cheeks as she cried like a thrashed child half her age. Pauline looked into her eyes and smiled, and for well over a minute gleefully licked the tears as they flowed down, one after the other, seemingly without cessation. She smacked her lips to savour the salty taste, ensuring that the anguished girl could watch her enjoyment close-up.

Finally sated, Pauline stood up straight.

"All right, cry-baby. Down on your knees."

Dolly obeyed, still shaking and sniffling, and got off the armchair to kneel down in front of her Mistress. She looked up, waiting for instructions. Her bottom stung terribly, but she didn't dare touch it.

"Now say it!"

"Th-thank you, Paulie. Thank you for correcting me." Another trembling sniffle.

"You get what you deserve…" intoned Pauline.

"And I deserve what I get," responded Dolly.

"Correct. Now the kisses."

"How many? I can't remember…"

"Nine strokes. That's all you could take. Not even double figures. Pretty feeble, aren't you?"

"Yes. I'm sorry. I'll try harder – I'll try to be stronger next time."

"Go on then… nine loving kisses for Paulie's magic wand."

Slowly, with extreme tenderness, Dolly planted nine kisses along the rattan cane as Pauline held it to her face. She was still breathing heavily.

Pauline smiled, basking in her triumph. Her voice softened.

"Do you love me, Sweetheart?"

Dolly looked up at her again.

"Yes, Paulie. I love you."

"Say it again."

"I love you, Paulie!"

Pauline held out her hand, and Dolly kissed the back of it adoringly; then she rubbed her wet face all over it like an affectionate kitten. Finally she looked up at her Mistress with a sweet blissful smile, despite her bleary eyes. Her submission was complete. Pauline was exhilarated by the sight.

"Dolly, you're so beautiful."

"You're beautiful too, Paulie."

Pauline beamed and felt like a goddess, radiating light and power in all directions.

"So who's the Queen?"

"You're the Queen, Paulie. Always and forever."

## II

## AFTER-EFFECTS

THE MORNING AFTER Midsummer Eve was bright and sunny and the woods to the west of St Margaret's School were drenched in golden emerald. The coupé wound its way up an incline along a narrow country lane, with Philip at the wheel and Annabel navigating from a road map. Eventually the car pulled over into a rough lay-by and they got out. Both were dressed in t-shirts and denim shorts.

"There it is," said Annabel, pointing to a footpath some twenty yards ahead. "That takes us to the gorge."

"Have you been this way before?" asked Philip.

"No. My previous visit started from the School. A special excursion, you might say…"

As they entered the footpath, Annabel reached for his hand. The ground was hard and dry, unlike the previous time, and the air was caressingly warm. Ideal conditions for a return visit. High up in the shining trees the birds sang happily and made her feel welcome. After only a hundred yards she heard in the distance the murmur of the river, this time much quieter and slower. Nonetheless she clung to Philip's hand as they approached the gorge.

The old bridge was bathed in morning sunshine, which gave it a rich mellow hue. It looked serene and harmless. An elderly couple with a dog greeted them as they passed by, coming from the woods on the opposite side of the gorge. Then they were on the bridge and Annabel looked down over the parapet at the clear sunlit water tinkling by – so much shallower and calmer than she remembered it. The river was now no more than two or three feet deep. The view downstream was as scenic as before. The steep banks were more thickly overgrown and the granite embankment on the right was almost entirely covered in billowing shrubs and gigantic weeds. The crude stone stairway that led down to it had likewise disappeared under shrubbery. She was relieved to see that the embankment was to all intents and purposes inaccessible.

"What a great view!" exclaimed Philip.

"Phil, would you stay where you are for a minute? I just want to go to that spot over there and meditate."

"Sure." He looked perplexed. Annabel was not the meditating type.

She had now identified the exact part of the parapet on which she had stood, naked and terrified, when ordered by Pauline to dive into the river. Tentatively she walked a few yards over to it and placed her hands on the very stones which had supported her feet. She ran her hands over them and was astonished by their roughness. No wonder her feet had been cut and bleeding afterwards. She pressed down and felt one of the heavy grey stones shift under her hand. The pointing was now crumbling away and it was unlikely the parapet could safely support anyone's weight.

Annabel looked down again into the river, trying to locate the precise spot where she had struck the water. She called over to Philip.

"Phil, how big would you say is the drop from the bridge?"

"How far down? Oh, I'd say about twenty feet at least."

She recalled the trajectory of her dive, which she had made as lengthy as possible to reduce the depth of the water required to absorb the impact of her body. How far was it? At least five yards along… suddenly she spied a squat irregular knoll on the river bed, covered in exotic dark green weeds that undulated slowly as the river ran over them. It had been invisible when she had dived in, because the rushing turbulent water was then twice as deep. But she knew at once that this was what had struck her abdomen as she hit the water, just below her navel, and had made her scream out with pain. Afterwards she had carried a large heavy bruise at the point of impact, which took weeks to disappear. The abdominal pains lasted for at least two months, and would grind into her bowels at various times of the day and wake her abruptly at night: she frequently had to curl up in bed and bite her pillow to avoid crying out and waking her room-mates in the dormitory. She felt unable to go to Matron for help because then she would have had to explain how she had received the injury. She recalled that the worry-worm had started to afflict her during the time she took her exams at the end of the fifth year, shortly after the grinding pains had faded. Was the worm a physiological after-effect of her injury or a psychological reaction to it? She had never suffered from it before the incident, and since then it had afflicted her whenever she felt under emotional pressure. As the years went by and she married Andrew and failed to fall pregnant, she began to wonder whether the injury had also destroyed her ability to conceive. She had sought medical advice and been examined by several gynaecologists. Scans had shown that her ovaries were scarred and afflicted with adhesions, and this was very likely the cause of her infertility. It was impossible to confirm medically whether her schoolgirl injury was responsible for her damaged ovaries, but deep down she had always felt that it was. No-one else in her family, on either her father's or her mother's side, had suffered from infertility. This was the reason for the collapse of her marriage to Andrew, who had wanted children and gave up on her after six years when it was apparent that she would never conceive. She knew that the differences between them had stemmed from this problem, and therefore she blamed herself for the marital breakdown. Andrew had since remarried and was now the father of a young son. Her numerous affairs since the divorce were in part a desperate attempt to compensate for her previous failure – as if the more sex she had, the more likely it was that she might finally fall pregnant. She feared that her relationship with Philip would founder for the same reason, as he had made it clear that he wanted to settle down with her and have children. She had told him about her infertility but of course not the suspected cause of it. So far he had been patient, but after eight months of intense coupling without the desired outcome she was growing concerned that he might start to lose interest. He was a man who liked to get results. She had been the same, hungry for success and achievement, but in recent years had had to accept that at the most fundamental level in life she had failed...

"Don't you think you've had enough meditation, my love?" said Philip, arriving at her side. "It doesn't seem to have made you very happy. Just the opposite, I would say."

"Sorry," she replied, smiling languidly. "Lots of old memories."

"Can you share them with me?" He put his arm around her waist.

She grimaced and shook her head. "Not yet. Maybe later."

"Oh well, as a matter of fact I was doing some meditation myself. I was meditating on how the sunshine makes your skin glow like warm honey. It looks good enough to lick... all over."

He lowered his hand over her blue denim shorts and began squeezing her backside.

"Not here, Phil. This isn't the right place or the right time..."

"Then you shouldn't wear such tight shorts and a t-shirt that shows off your beautiful boobs. In fact, you shouldn't be so damn sexy."

"Phil – what can we do on this bridge? People are passing by every five minutes..."

"I wasn't thinking of here on the bridge. What about that thick patch of trees we passed by a minute ago, just off the footpath? It looks nice and cosy. The ground is dry. You like a bit of outdoor sex now and again."

"My God, I can't believe you're still randy after you had me so many times last night. You saw the looks we got from some of the hotel guests at breakfast this morning."

"It's your fault. You make me randy all the time." He kissed her cheek and then pushed his big hand down inside the back of her shorts, spreading his warmth over one of her buttocks.

"All right, but not here. Not in these woods."

"Where then?"

"In the car. Somewhere far from here. I'm sure we can find a secluded spot along the journey."

"I suppose so. But I feel horny right now. What's wrong with this place?"

Annabel sighed and withdrew his hand from her shorts.

"All right then, if you must know: I got fucked here many years ago, and I don't fancy a repeat episode. You know, bad vibes…"

Philip's face dropped.

"Bloody hell! I think I need to learn a bit more about what you got up to at school!"

She smiled at his reaction, and took his hand in hers.

"I think I need to learn a bit more as well. Come on, let's go back to the car."

As they moved away, she looked down at the water one last time. The knoll looked like a dark green octopus lurking on the riverbed, lying in wait for its next victim.


The photo-lights blazed all over Pauline's studio, saturating the ancient white-painted brick walls with brilliant silver.

Completely naked, Dolly knelt on a large cushion with her thighs open at the customary angle. She looked back over her shoulder at Pauline, who was still adjusting her camera, mounted on a tripod.

"Is this right, Paulie?"

"Almost, Sweetheart. You just need to face forward and straighten your back so the light falls properly on that perfect arse. I want those stripes to stand out nice and clear."

"Do they look good?" Dolly turned to face front as instructed.

"Yes, a lovely shade of purple. They look so… *emphatic* against your white skin. This time I've got exactly the pattern I wanted – a nice even distribution over both cheeks. I think this is going to be the best of the Lovelines so far. I should get a decent price for it."

"I'm glad you're pleased. It really hurt this time. I've never known you cane me so hard."

"Sorry Sweetheart, but I was turned on by that School Reunion party."

Dolly looked round again.

"What turned you on? Was it Annabel?"

Pauline looked up from the camera and grinned.

"How did you guess?"

"You were right – she really is fucking gorgeous."

"Now face front, Sweetheart, or I'm going to have to thrash you somewhere else – where it hurts a lot more."

Dolly instantly obeyed. She knew it was no idle threat.

Pauline started snapping the camera and Dolly's exquisite bottom was once again recorded for posterity. Or posteriority, as Pauline liked to call it. The next *Lovelines* template was in the bag, ready for conversion to gaudy silkscreen. An artist had to make a living somehow.

# III

# PROPOSITIONS

THE WEEKLY CASE MEETING in the Stroke Unit was finally drawing to a close. The nine members of Annabel's team – doctors, nurses, physiotherapists, occupational therapists – sat around a large table. All of them were showing signs of fatigue, worn down by a particularly gruelling last few days. The hot weather in this last week of June wasn't helping.

"OK folks," said Annabel. "Last three cases, I think. Pete, can you go through these for us?"

Peter, one of Annabel's assistant physicians in the team, looked at his notes.

"Deborah Hemmings, aged seventy-eight. Haemorrhage six weeks ago. Partial recovery after intensive treatment. Recommended for transfer to Rehab, followed by occupational therapy and eventual discharge for return to home."

"What are the OT prospects?" asked Annabel.

"Not good," said Mike, the therapist. "Owing to age and disability. I'd say very dubious recovery prospects."

"All right," said Annabel, "I examined Mrs Hemmings two days ago and I understand your pessimism. But I think she's improved in the last week and since she still has her husband living with her, I think we have to try to return her home after appropriate rehab. I want her to have at least six weeks at the clinic before we make a final decision. Next one?"

"Robert Gordon, aged eighty-one. Temporary ischaemic attack ten days ago, fairly minor clot, now showing definite signs of recovery."

Annabel nodded, adjusting the band of her pony tail, which had started to work loose. It had been a long shift.

"Yes, I think Mr Gordon looks fit to return home. Let's keep him here for three more days before discharge. Because of his age, I'd like to see follow-up reports for at least two months. Is that OK, Jane?"

"Yes," replied Jane, making a note. "I'll make sure we get them."

"Fine. Last one, Pete?"

"Gwen Simpson. Age thirty-six. Severe brain haemorrhage following car accident. Still in coma. No sign of improvement."

An air of gloomy resignation spread around the table. Several of the team stared down at their notes.

"No improvement at all?" asked Annabel.

"No," said Sunita, another of Annabel's assistant physicians. She was a young doctor in her mid-twenties. "I've been working on this case for the past week and as far as I can see, the bleeding is getting worse all the time. Today her condition has deteriorated, as these tests show, and I don't see any chance of recovery. In my opinion the prognosis is terminal."

"How long?" asked Annabel.

Sunita shrugged. "I'd say no more than a couple of days. Could be even less. Maybe just a matter of hours."

"I think you're right," nodded Annabel. "What about her family?"

"No husband. Single mother. Older son no longer at home. There's just her daughter, aged fifteen, who's here at the hospital with the patient's sister. They've been waiting around for news for several hours. Obviously the girl is in a bit of a state."

"Has anyone seen them?" asked Annabel.

"I did see them, yesterday," replied Sunita, "but… I haven't had time to give them the latest news."

There was a pause.

"Do you want me to talk to them?" asked Sunita.

Annabel considered for a moment. She looked at her young assistant and shook her head.

"No, I'll see them myself. Leave it to me."

"Thank you, Annabel," said Sunita quietly. "I really appreciate that."

From a distance the girl and her aunt were quickly recognisable in the largely empty waiting room, occupying two of the cold plastic seats. They were numb after days of waiting and expecting the worst. The girl looked a little younger than fifteen. She had long light brown hair and wore a black top and a tartan skirt, similar in pattern to the one Dolly had worn at the Reunion party, though nothing like as recklessly short. Her eyes were swollen and she fidgeted with a magazine in her lap.

Annabel smoothed down her blue staff tunic and walked over to the pair.

"Hello – I'm Doctor James, senior consultant in the Stroke Unit. Are you Gwen Simpson's family?"

She shook hands with the aunt, who nodded and briefly rose to her feet.

"Any news, doctor?"

Annabel took the seat next to the girl, who looked at her with huge eyes.

"Are you Katie?"

The girl nodded slowly.

"Katie – I'm sorry, but I have to tell you it looks as if your mother isn't going to come round. We ran more tests a few hours ago and sadly we couldn't see any sign of recovery. The bleeding in her brain has got worse."

The girl turned and sank her head in her aunt's chest. She began to heave with sobs.

Annabel leaned over and took her hand.

"I'm so sorry, Katie. If it's any comfort at all, I know what you're feeling right now."

A little surprised, the girl turned to look at her. Tears darted down her cheeks. Annabel knew that her personal history was surplus to requirements, but she was moved by the girl's anguish.

"When I was nineteen my father died in a car crash. He was gone within hours of being taken to hospital and I remember being in a waiting room just like this when they brought me the bad news."

Katie's crying stopped. This had grabbed her attention.

"It all seemed so cruel and senseless," continued Annabel. "I was very close to my father – he was always the most important person in my life – and I just couldn't believe what had happened. For a while I didn't know how to go on."

"At least you had the rest of your family," replied Katie, in a tone of mild protest.

"Yes, I did. But my mother then had a breakdown and my young brother refused to speak to anyone for ages. I had to look after both of them for quite a while."

"How did you do that?"

"I decided to take on all the good qualities my father had – his courage, his strength, his care for his family – because I realised the best way of remembering him was to keep him alive inside myself, and to show his qualities to others. If he was still watching me from some other world, I wanted him to be proud of me. That's what kept me going."

Katie stared at her.

"I'm sure you're proud of your mother, Katie, if she brought you up on her own for years."

There was a nod of assent. Annabel gently squeezed her hand.

"So now make her proud of you. Remind the rest of your family of what she was by the way you behave to them. It's the best tribute to her that you could make. And it's the best way for you to come through this terrible time."

Still staring fixedly at Annabel, Katie nodded again. She was thinking hard.

The aunt smiled at Annabel.

"Thank you doctor. Thank you so much."

Annabel released Katie's hand.

"I'll make sure someone sees you again in couple of hours," she said, rising to go.

"Doctor – did your mum and brother get better?" asked Katie.

"Yes," said Annabel, with a consoling smile. "Eventually we all recovered. And so will you."

As she walked away, Annabel resolved that she would see Dolly again.

It was early July and the mid-afternoon weather in London was hot and humid. To stay cool, Annabel wore a thin yellow shirt dress as she strolled along Brick Lane, passing through the pungent aromas of the curry-houses. She turned into one of the side streets. The tall Georgian townhouses retained their old sinister glamour despite the area's gentrification, and were still redolent of the days of the Ripper. She checked the address on her card and found a dark narrow alleyway, signposted "Black Sun Gallery". A little apprehensive, she paused. The worry-worm was at work again. But it was too late to turn back: she had accepted the invitation and would go through with the encounter.

She entered the high-walled alleyway and after some ten yards found on her right a black-painted double-door entrance, with a sign above it showing a spinning black vortex on a white background. The foyer within was brightly lit, with a burly young black man behind a desk acting as both reception and security guard.

Annabel gave him her name. He looked at a note on his desk.

"Ah, Miss James. You're expected. Just a moment." He picked up a phone.

Annabel looked at a large poster on the wall declaring "Superreal Women: New Exhibition by Pauline Barrie". It featured a cartoon of an alarmingly muscular woman raising a flesh-coloured truncheon which on second glance turned out to be a stylised penis.

The receptionist put down the phone, and after a few moments Dolly emerged from within. She was dressed in a short white toga costume, based on classical Greek design, with shoulder straps made of gold cord and a similar cord tied tightly around the slender waist, raising the toga's hem perilously high. The long side slits rising from the hem to her hip on both sides showed that she was once again bereft of underwear. A braided gold headband and gold sandals completed the picture. As before, her face was heavily made up. It seemed to Annabel that she was always dressed up, never really dressed. But she was totally enchanting as she came forward, smiling eagerly, pale hand outstretched.

"Annabel – it's lovely to see you again!"

They shook hands warmly. Annabel's apprehension was dispelled.

"Pleased to see you, Dolly. You look so pretty. Are you going to be my guide?"

"Yes, Pauline asked me to show you around. She'll be along shortly."

As they entered the main gallery, which was spacious and modern and brightly lit, and empty apart from them, Annabel's attention was immediately drawn to the large figure in the centre, raised on a waist-high plinth, a lifelike model of a naked girl crouching on roller skates rendered in what looked like smooth white resin or fibreglass. The model's dark hair streamed backwards horizontally for almost four feet to give a dramatic impression of break-neck speed as she whizzed along on the skates, which were coloured jet black. Her arms were open wide, as if embracing the onrushing wind, and there was an ecstatic trance-like expression on her face. Ignoring everything else, Annabel walked straight over to this exhibit. As she examined the model's face, she realised that it was Dolly. The features had been reproduced with remarkable accuracy and were unmistakably hers. On the base of the exhibit was a placard: "A Girl's Destiny".

"What do you think?" said Dolly, following up behind her.

"Why, it's breath-taking," replied Annabel after a brief pause. "Most impressive. I had no idea Pauline was doing this kind of work."

As she walked slowly around the figure, Annabel noted the minute attention to detail which had gone into the construction of the model. It was an exact, fully life-sized replica of Dolly. And it was clearly a labour of love. She turned to the girl.

"Dolly, I can see you're a star already. She's caught you so well. The expression on your face is wonderful. It just… lifts me up inside. Makes me remember what it was like to be a girl."

"I'd love to have seen you as a girl," said Dolly, putting her arm in Annabel's. "Come on, let me show you around." Annabel made no attempt to disengage her arm. She could smell the musky perfume again.

The walls were covered with a variety of colourful paintings and silkscreens but Annabel's attention stayed fixed on the sculptural exhibits. On a small table was a life-sized female abdominal section, with perfectly shaped smooth white belly and buttocks, which was impaled on a thick shiny black vertical penis, half-buried in the model's vaginal shaft. The work was labelled, somewhat superfluously, "Going Down".

Annabel raised an eyebrow and looked pointedly at Dolly.

"I think I recognise that bottom. Did you model this piece as well?"

"Oh yes," replied Dolly. "Paulie likes to work from a live body. She calls it Life-casting."

"And the black shaft?"

"Oh that was a dildo, not an actual guy. I'm not really into guys, if I have a choice..."

Dolly held her arm tighter and Annabel became aware of her own breathing.

"Are there any other models of you?"

"Yes, a few, but not just me. Look over here."

Somewhat to Annabel's relief, Dolly took her to several exhibits which were obviously based on larger, heavier, older women. All of them showed the same fetishistic attention to the nude female form, and many were humorous and warm-hearted: a plump figure called "Homage to Auntie Flo" caught her attention, as did a grossly swollen abdomen giving birth to a lurid red baby with horns on its head and a devilish grin on its face.

Dolly looked conspiratorially at Annabel.

"Paulie is working on something at the moment which she says is going to be her masterpiece. She's been at it now for a few weeks, over in her studio in Whitechapel."

"Is it modelled on you?" asked Annabel.

"No, it's going to be based on someone else. She won't tell me any more about it until she's finished it. She says her work is going in a new direction which takes her back to her Roman Catholic childhood. Paulie's a bit of a weirdo, you know. She's really into magic and sorcery and all that stuff. She says it gives her inspiration for her artwork. Do you have any religious beliefs?"

"Not any more. I was brought up as a Roman Catholic, which is why I went to St Margaret's, just like Pauline. As a scientist, I can't subscribe to the Catholic Faith. But I still believe in Christian morality – and I'd like to think there's some kind of God."

"A God who loves us?"

"Yes, a God who loves us, despite our faults."

"I can't believe you have any faults, Annabel."

"Oh, I can assure you I have," she laughed.

Dolly's hand slid down to squeeze Annabel's forearm as she looked at her with a mischievous grin.

"I'd love to know what they are…"

"Well… when you know me better, you may find out."

"I'm going to know you better – so I can find out everything about you!"

Annabel felt herself growing hot. The thin yellow dress began to cling to her body.

"Let's look at some of these paintings, shall we?"

They walked on and viewed the various paintings, all by Pauline, which featured the same type of subject-matter. Some were in oil, some in acrylic and some were garish silkscreens.

"I recognise that bottom yet again," said Annabel, archly. She inclined her head at a series of silkscreens featuring stripes criss-crossing a pair of buttocks in different colours and patterns.

"Yes, it's my bum again," smiled Dolly.

"What does the title mean? *Lovelines*?"

"Paulie thinks you always end up destroying the thing you love most. If you have something that's perfect, you can't stop yourself breaking it into smaller pieces. That's what the lines do. They break up the cuddly roundness of the bum-cheeks."

"They look a lot like cane strokes. Very realistic."

Dolly grinned. She licked her scarlet lips.

"Have you ever been caned, Annabel?"

"No, I can't say I have. What about you?"

"Of course I have. Lots of times. I'm a bad girl, so what do you expect?"

Annabel could feel the excitement coming through Dolly's slender hand as it slipped down and grasped hers. She drew a lengthy breath. But she allowed her hand to remain in Dolly's. She felt her knuckles brush against the hem of the white toga and found herself glancing down at the girl's upper thigh, exposed by the high side slit of the garment. Quickly she turned her attention to the silkscreens.

"Dolly – were you actually caned for these pictures to be made?"

Dolly put her forefinger to her lips and raised an eyebrow.

"Does that mean yes or no?" asked Annabel.

"Paulie says you always have to make sacrifices for Art," replied Dolly.

"And you're the sacrifice?"

"I've always been the sacrifice, for as long as I can remember."

"Do you enjoy that? I know there are people who do."

"I just accept it. It's what I am. I get what I deserve, and I deserve what I get."

Annabel held her hand tighter.

"My poor Dolly."

"Don't feel sorry for me. I'm not worth it."

"But of course you are…"

Without replying, Dolly turned and moved both hands down to grasp Annabel's.

"Paulie's coming," she whispered. "Please take this…"

Annabel felt a small piece of folded paper being pressed into the palm of her hand. Then Dolly abruptly disengaged herself. The sudden earnestness of her expression alerted Annabel, who discreetly put the paper in the chest pocket of her shirt dress.

Pauline was strolling towards them regally from the other side of the gallery. She wore a long silky pale coral dress that reached almost to her feet. For the first time, Annabel noticed the design on the floor, black sunrays on a white background widening and reaching out to the walls in every direction from a large black circle in the centre of the gallery. The floor gave Pauline's approach an oddly dramatic effect. This was the moment for which Annabel had been bracing herself…

Pauline was all charm as she arrived with a gracious smile and extended a long white hand with a huge black-stoned silver ring on the middle finger. Her big, slightly bulging blue eyes looked glazed and her pupils were unnaturally large – to Annabel, clear signs of recent drug use. The long cascade of red hair falling from her head and big circular ear-rings added to her strange appearance.

"Annabel! Thank you so much for taking the time to come and visit. I'm truly flattered."

Annabel shook the hand and mustered the warmest smile she could. She felt uneasy that Pauline, already taller than her, was wearing high heels to increase her height advantage.

"It's my pleasure, Pauline. Thank you for inviting me over for a special viewing."

"I trust Dolly has been keeping you occupied?"

"Oh yes – she's been a wonderful guide. I can see she's an inspiration for your work."

"Indeed she is – a constant inspiration."

Dolly was smiling up at Pauline in an ecstasy of adoration. Annabel wondered whether this was a role that she was always required to play in their relationship, at least whenever a third party was present.

"Sweetheart," said Pauline to Dolly, "Rickie has just arrived at reception and needs to be entertained for a while. Go over and keep him company until I'm ready for him." She reached under Dolly's short toga and lightly but audibly slapped her bare bottom, at the same time inclining her head towards the foyer. A large rotund middle-aged man with a heavy beard was nodding and waving at them from the other end of the gallery.

"Yes Paulie, right away," beamed Dolly, as if being seen to obey the orders of her Mistress were the greatest pleasure in her life. She shook hands with Annabel, looking at her still with that expression of blissful obedience, and then marched off towards the foyer as commanded.

"Rickie is Richard Squire," explained Pauline. "He's an influential art journalist I've been cultivating for quite a while. I feed him Dolly from time to time to keep him happy."

Annabel decided to ignore the implications of this remark.

"You seem to have Dolly very much in hand, if you'll pardon me saying so."

Pauline continued to smile regally. She was obviously proud of her ascendancy over the girl.

"As you probably know, Dolly's had a wild and wayward childhood. So now she loves to get the discipline she's always lacked. She thrives on it. It's made a much better person of her."

"She seems delighted to be with you."

"I'll let you into a little secret," said Pauline. "Dolly isn't her real name at all. It's a name I gave to her, to help her put her past identity behind her. She's happier being Dolly, my creature, than whatever she was before."

"How intriguing. What was her name before?"

Pauline shook her head.

"Nobody who knows her now will ever find out what her previous name was. She's under strict orders never to disclose it to anyone. She understands it's for her own good. Let's say it's an experiment in mental reprogramming."

"Is mental reprogramming something you specialise in?"

"In a way, yes," replied Pauline, flattered by the question. "I have some… esoteric interests which involve mind control and reprogramming. I like to get into a trance state before I do any work – I need to sink down into the subconscious level of my mind before I can create anything worthwhile. You know, invoke the demon within."

"It's certainly been successful," said Annabel. "You've produced some impressive work, from what I can see here. I like the sculptures, if that's the right term for them. They're very… provocative."

"You have to be provocative to get noticed at all these days," smiled Pauline. "My work is in the tradition of an art movement called Super Realism, which goes all the way back to Pop Art and even Surrealism. It breaks down the barriers between Art and Reality, so ultimately you can't tell one from the other. I enhance and exaggerate the human body, to try to make people think about themselves in a different way. I like to strip down the personality to its bare essence, in order to bring out its 'Super Reality', to show what it truly *is*. I want to show the human soul completely naked. Hence the stress on the nude body."

"I love the sculpture over there which shows Dolly on roller-skates. She looks well and truly stripped down."

Pauline chuckled. They strolled over to view "A Girl's Destiny".

"Yes, this is one of my favourite pieces," continued Pauline, touching the statue's buttock. "I'm currently exploring the nostalgias of childhood to produce a new kind of work. This time with a big religious theme."

"What's your theme?"

"The Artist as God, and God as Artist. God spends his time creating a multitude of things and then destroys every last one of them – as if He created them in the first place just to have the pleasure of destroying them. In my view the Artist should do the same, or at least reveal God for what He really is. The ultimate Sadist."

"That's a harsh view of the world."

"But it's true – as far as I see it. What's your view of the world?"

Annabel paused before replying.

"I think that… whatever lies in the human heart must be reflected out there on some grand cosmic level. There's plenty of cruelty but also plenty of love."

"But that's my point," smiled Pauline. "In the end you can't separate one from the other. They're both part of the same process!"

Annabel shrugged.

"God as Divine Sadist? I'll have to give that one some thought."

"In any case," smiled Pauline, "it suits me to think that way, as an artist who likes to play God."

"Dolly said you were working on your masterpiece."

"Yes. I think it'll be the most powerful thing I've done to date. It's time I reached back to my past self… back to my earliest childhood years."

Pauline suddenly turned to face Annabel. Her voice deepened.

"Annabel, I'm so pleased you accepted my peace offering from Dolly at the School Reunion."

"It seemed the right thing to do, after so many years."

"I treated you horribly that day on the bridge. As time has gone by I've felt worse and worse about it, and I couldn't rest any more until I'd made the effort to contact you. That's really why I went to the Reunion Party."

"I realise that."

Pauline touched Annabel's hand. She seemed intensely sincere.

"Can you find a way to forgive me for what I did?"

"Yes. Otherwise I wouldn't be here now."

"What I did was based on jealousy and crazy schoolgirl obsession. You know I had a terrible crush on you."

"That was obvious." Annabel was again conscious of her own breathing. Pauline withdrew her hand.

"You were the most beautiful and the most perfect girl I had ever seen, and I desperately wanted you to myself just for an hour. I knew you'd never want to be my friend so I had to find some way of forcing you to be alone with me and do what I wanted. I couldn't overcome you by fair means so I had to resort to foul means. It was a terrible thing to do – making you jump from that bridge."

"It almost killed me," said Annabel, wincing at the memory. "I really thought I was going to be swept away."

"I would never have let you perish," said Pauline. "You meant far too much to me. Seeing you now, I'm so glad you're still fit and healthy and doing well. I hear you're a successful doctor."

Though pleased by Pauline's friendly attitude, Annabel remained cautious.

"To be honest, it's hard to see yourself as successful in the medical profession. I manage to do the best I can for as many people as I can. Maybe that counts as success."

"You're still a shining example to me, just as you were at school. I'd like to make it up to you somehow, for what I did to you back then. You won't be offended if I suggest something?"

"I doubt it."

"I'd love to use you for a model, just as I've used Dolly for this piece here. I'd like to make a sculpture of you with a hockey stick, running forward in full flow. I'd call it… 'Miss Perfect'. It would be magnificent!"

"Well – what an idea!" Annabel was taken aback, and momentarily excited by the proposition. She looked again at the smooth impermeable white body of the roller-skater beside her.

"What would I need to do?" she asked.

"I'd have to take a number of photographs of you... without any clothing. You'd have to pose nude with that hockey stick in my studio. I'd need those images to work on the model."

"Life-casting?"

"Yes, that's it."

Annabel thought for a moment.

"I'm flattered by your proposal, and I can see what a fine piece of work you'd produce."

"Annabel – you'd be immortalised!"

"I appreciate what you're saying. It's very tempting. But I want my naked body to be reserved for my lovers. And for the sports changing-room! I'm sorry – I know it makes me sound terribly dull – but I'll have to turn down your kind offer. Even if it means I miss out on immortality."

Pauline's face fell, though only slightly. Clearly she had trained herself to retain her composure, even on those rare occasions when she didn't get her way.

"Oh, what a shame! I remember how beautiful your body looked on the bridge, even in the most... trying circumstances. I'd so love to turn it into a work of art. But never mind..."

Annabel strove to be conciliatory.

"Pauline, it means a lot to me that you've made this proposition. It's a great compliment. I like the idea of being on a plinth and being admired – who wouldn't? But really, it just isn't me. I'm sorry to be so negative."

Pauline beamed at her, albeit with tight jaws.

"No need to apologise! You've just proved to me what a principled woman you are!"

She leaned over and kissed Annabel on the cheek, then stepped back to admire her. Annabel was surprised to see tears in her eyes. They were still glazed, the pupils still enlarged.

"To me, Annabel, you'll always be Miss Perfect! Forever!"

Shortly afterwards, on the tube train back to Earls Court, Annabel unfolded and read the scrap of paper that Dolly had surreptitiously passed to her.

*Please help me. Call me on this number.*
*Dolly*

## IV

## STORM CLOUDS

IT WAS THE NIGHT of the Full Moon. Incense swirled eagerly out of the antique bronze burner and curled up towards the high ceiling of Pauline's studio, now shrouded in darkness. The only light came from the large black candles that burned on tall wrought-iron stands on either side of a six-foot high silkscreen mounted on a metal frame. The screen showed a monstrous black dragon over a white background, its fearsome jaws wide open and its arms and wings outstretched with predatory intent. Its long tail trailed downwards in viperous coils. Facing the screen from a short distance was Pauline, dressed in a black gown and sitting bolt upright on a black iron chair. Immediately in front of her was a small round table with a black velvet cloth draped over it. A deck of well-worn Tarot cards was neatly stacked, face down, waiting to be dealt.

The grandfather clock at the back of the studio struck twelve times.

As soon as midnight had been sounded, Pauline pronounced the invocation in a slow, intense, vibrating monotone.

*To Arxegono Fidi*
*To Megalo Drako*
*O Opoios eitan kai*
*O Opoios enai*
*O Aionas ton Aionon*
*Einai me ton pneuma sou!*

She reached for the Tarot deck and shuffled the cards, eyes firmly shut, repeatedly muttering "To Megalo Drako!" After approximately a minute she stopped and replaced the deck face down on the table. She opened her eyes, breathed deeply and took the top card from the pile. She turned it and laid it down slightly to the left of the centre of the table. It signified the Past.

*Queen of Swords.*

Pauline nodded. This made sense.

She took the second card, again from the top of the pile, and laid it to the right of the first one, in the dead centre of the table. The Present.

*The Lovers.*

She smiled wryly and nodded again.

Then she took the third card, and laid it to the right of the other two. The Future.

*Ten of Swords.*

Pauline frowned and slowly shook her head. This was disturbing. One more card was required.

She cut the pack roughly halfway down and from the re-arranged stack took the top card. This was the Supernal, the Overriding Power which influenced all the others. She placed it above the line of three cards she had previously drawn and turned it over.

*The Blasted Tower.*

Pauline took a deep breath and groaned. She hung her head. There were no more cards left to play.

The weather had now become so hot and heavy that a thunderstorm had been forecast for the afternoon. The green tarmac surface of the tennis court roasted in the sunshine and almost seemed to slow down the ball as it bounced from one side of the court to the other. Annabel and Philip were at their west London club for a doubles match against another couple, who were slightly younger. As per the club's rule, everyone was dressed entirely in white. The match was part of a competition and was for the best of three sets. All the participants hoped to complete it before the predicted storm arrived.

In the third and final set Annabel's athleticism and technique finally proved decisive, as she sent one winning shot after another down the tramlines. She finished with an overhead smash which drew applause from the dozen or so spectators who were watching.

The defeated couple shook hands and departed for the club-house, along with the spectators. Annabel and Philip, both hot and weary, sat on two of the plastic chairs at the side of the now-empty court to recover their breath. They dabbed themselves with towels to wipe away their perspiration.

"You were brilliant!" puffed Philip. "The oldest player on the court and you made mincemeat of them. I'm very impressed. How do you do it?"

Annabel exhaled heavily and pulled her visor down to keep the sun out of her face. She rubbed her towel over her brown thighs, which were covered in sweat.

"I don't like to be beaten," she replied. "Something I inherited from my father. He always told me to save my strength, mentally, for the crucial moment – when the others start getting tired and lose concentration."

"You must miss your father."

"Oh, I really do. I still can't believe he's no longer here, even after so many years."

"Were you at university when it happened?"

"Yes, I was in my first year. It disrupted everything so much I only just passed my exams at the end of the year."

"How's your mother doing?"

Annabel stared at the tarmac as she continued to wipe herself with the towel.

"Not great. She's still knocking back the gin and tonic throughout the day. She starts pretty much as soon as she gets up in the morning."

"And your brother?"

She shook her head.

"I hardly ever hear from him these days. I guess he's OK, out there in Japan. He can forget about his past and be somebody else."

Philip put his hand on her knee. She lifted off her visor. In the distance, above the trees at the perimeter of the tennis club, she saw a dark cloud suddenly appear. The thunderstorm was coming.

"Bella, you must get lonely and depressed sometimes. Your friends can only do so much for you. I'd love to give you the support you deserve. Don't you think it's time we got together full-time? I mean, got hitched up properly?"

Annabel continued to stare at the ground as she undid the band holding her pony-tail and shook her hair loose. She let out another long breath.

"Phil, I know how much you care for me and I appreciate everything you do – and everything you can offer. But I'm an independent girl. I really enjoy my freedom, especially after being married for six years. The only thing that would make me want to live with a man was having his child. Then I'd be happy to get hitched up properly."

Philip paused to consider his reply. He sensed that Annabel didn't want to continue with the conversation but felt that now was the time to pursue the matter. He turned to look at her.

"Darling – I know you're far from old, but isn't it time you investigated this pregnancy thing properly? I mean, if you're serious about having kids one day. Thirty-six isn't exactly a young age to start motherhood, even these days."

Annabel raised her towel and began to wipe the sweat from her hair. She avoided looking back at him.

"What do you want me to do, Phil?"

"Well, aren't there clinics you can visit to see about artificial fertility and surrogate pregnancy and so on? It's obvious that normal sex isn't having any effect, however much we do it. There has to be something else we can try. That is, if you're serious about wanting children."

She made no reply but continued wiping her hair. The cloud above the trees was rapidly growing larger and heavier and darker.

Philip squeezed her thigh.

"Bella – you are serious, aren't you?"

"Phil, I am serious about you but I have to be honest – I don't know if I want to settle down yet, with you or anyone else. I know I'm not emotionally... fulfilled, but that's because I don't really know what I want. But right now the prospect of another marriage doesn't fill me with joy and excitement. I'm sorry, but that's the way I feel."

Philip sighed loudly and shook his head. This hit him almost with the force of a betrayal. Slowly he withdrew his hand from her thigh.

"Bella – I don't know what more I can say. I thought we were really going somewhere."

She put her towel around her shoulders.

"You mustn't try to push me where I don't want to go, Phil. I can't let another person turn me into something I'm not."

Philip scowled. She could see he was growing exasperated – angry, even. She tried to lighten the mood.

"Remember I'm a St Margaret's girl!"

"Huh! To hell with St Margaret's!"

At this moment the first gust of cool wind reached them, moving surprisingly fast, and the sun was abruptly blotted out by the expanding thundercloud, which had turned almost black. There was a distant rumble of thunder.

"Storm's going to hit us in a minute," said Philip, grimacing. "We'd better get back to the club-house. We need some liquid refreshment anyway."

He rose to his feet and reached for his kit-bag. On adjoining courts players and spectators were now scurrying away to seek shelter.

As Annabel gazed at the approaching thundercloud, a thrilling impulse suddenly took hold of her. She recalled the sculpture of Dolly on rollerskates that she had viewed in the Black Sun Gallery three days earlier: A Girl's Destiny. She recalled how the Girl's long hair trailed behind her, like a huge black brushstroke rendered by an almighty hand. She realised that she was now yearning for a new direction and felt, however absurdly, that the thunderstorm could show her which way to go. The prospect of its power and authority was enthralling. It was like a new lover coming to take her.

"You go back, Phil. I want to stay here."

He was dumbfounded.

"What? Stay out here in the thunderstorm? You can't be serious! Just look at the damn thing coming at us!"

She smiled at him; a strange thin vacant smile that he had never seen before.

"I'll be fine, really. I'm so hot – I badly need to cool off."

"Cool off? You'll be drowned if you stay out here! Now come on – it's going to hit us in another minute!"

The wind was now whistling angrily through the air and making the net in the middle of the court sway agitatedly. Annabel felt her hair start to lift as the wind struck her face.

"You must be crazy!" shouted Philip. He hastily put his towel in his kit-bag and zipped it shut.

Annabel continued to smile at him. She couldn't believe her own serenity. She felt utterly calm. There was no sign of the worry-worm. None at all.

"Annabel, one last time – come on, please!"

She slowly shook her head at him.

"All right – have it your way!" Philip cursed under his breath before turning and running from the court, just as the first drops of rain came down. Annabel felt the spots peppering her head, then her shoulders and chest and legs. The abrupt coolness was a relief.

As she waited for the storm to hit her, she thought about Dolly. Had the girl received her phone call? Annabel had rung her on the number written on the scrap of paper on the evening of her visit to the gallery, and had left a spoken message for her, giving Dolly her own telephone number. What danger was she in? What oppression or degradation was Pauline subjecting her to? Was she even free to reply to the message? What more could she do to help her?

Then came the first lightning flash, striking with astonishing vividness somewhere in the trees ahead of her. This was followed by a hard muscular crack of thunder, which seemed to shake the tennis court. It reminded her of the roars of the lions that she had heard in the zoo when she was taken there as a child by her father.

A Girl's Destiny… she opened her arms and waited for the impact…

After a few seconds came the first real shower, whistling and swishing down at her with a ferocious zeal and instantly soaking her all over. She opened her arms wider to welcome the wetness, pushing her chest forward; then she opened her thighs as wide as they could stretch and leaned back until she was in danger of slipping off the front of the chair. She looked down through the cascade of water and saw that her tennis dress was already drenched and clearly revealing the flesh of her midriff and the white of her bra. She tugged forward the top of the dress to let the rain pour in over her cleavage. Then she lifted the hem of the dress up and back to allow the water to rush freely onto her white sports briefs; in a moment they too were completely soaked, showing the dark patch of her pubic hair. She could even feel the rain now washing under her backside. In the seat of the plastic chair a pool had formed. She sat back and writhed from side to side to allow her buttocks to open and let the water seep between them through the briefs. She wanted to be washed everywhere – washed clean.

Another lightning flash, this time nearer, followed by an immediate roar of thunder. It felt as if a huge winged monster was now closing in on her, preparing to devour her. But she trusted her courage at the crucial moment, as her father had always told her to, and remained calm and untroubled as the rain hissed and spattered at her body. The noise was deafening. She closed her eyes to protect them from the merciless shower. She was now overwhelmed by the downpour, completely defenceless. It was so heavy and so relentless that she even found it hard to draw breath. She wondered whether it was possible to drown in a rainstorm, if the air was replaced entirely by water.

The final flash struck immediately behind her, so close and so brilliant that she thought for a moment that she had been turned into thin air. At once a massive eruption of thunder came crashing down above her head and around her chair. The monster was full upon her, blasting its primal rage through her entire body. She was almost thrown off the chair but she gripped hard with her hands and her calves and somehow managed to stay upright. The windswept rain came down even harder than before, hammering at every part of her and almost blowing the hair off her head. But still she refused to break: she gritted her teeth and panted out the breaths, even though she was involuntarily trembling and quivering with the shock of it all. Her heart thumped fiercely. She glanced at the tarmac and saw the big rain-pennies sliding past her like an endless army of insects on the march. The net of the tennis court was almost horizontal under the pressure of the wind. Still she held on to herself, refusing to surrender to the monster as it buffeted her from different directions, varying the angle and the pace of its onslaught.

Then abruptly the storm turned away and left her. There was an exhalation – almost a sigh of dismay – as it gusted out of the tennis court and made its way towards the club-house a couple of hundred yards away. It was over, and she was still alive...

Annabel sat up straight. She was dazed yet exhilarated as she watched the departing storm. She had overcome it. Her clothing was so heavily saturated that she felt as if she weighed twice as much as she had before. Her hair hung down in a tangled mess of strands. It was hard even to move. She breathed long and deep to calm her pounding heart. Then the dark clouds slid silently away and the sun returned, slowly warming her with its golden smiling benevolence. She recalled Pauline's words about Super Realism and felt that she too had been stripped down to her bare essence by the storm; that she had been immeasurably strengthened by the experience and vindicated in her defiance. Sitting perfectly still and steady on her chair, not moving a muscle, she felt that she herself had become a work of art, a timeless statue just like the roller-skater in the gallery. A Girl's Destiny. She realised that a new path had opened up for her. She had no idea where it would lead, but she knew she was going to follow it.

Dolly gasped and sank to her knees. Thirteen!

She swallowed hard and tried to stop the sobbing. Another deep breath and a small tremor... then she felt she was more or less under control. She wiped the tears from her eyes and saw that Paulie was already holding out the cane in front of her face.

Thirteen! She was proud of herself. But it really hurt like hell, not just over her arse but over the back of her thighs. She wouldn't be able to show off her legs for at least a week after this beating.

"Now say it!" barked Pauline.

"Thank you, Paulie," said Dolly, smiling in her sweetest little-girlie manner. "Thank you for correcting me." She loved looking up at the long hard white naked body of her Mistress. Especially when she was also naked herself. And covered with red stripes. And filled with top-grade white powder.

"Now the kisses!"

"How many was it this time?" Dolly knew exactly how many but she wanted the Mistress to acknowledge her improvement.

"Thirteen. My lucky number! Well done, Dolly."

"You whacked my thighs this time. Fuck, it really hurts!"

"That's where the cane-demon takes me, Sweetheart. Now the kisses…"

Adoringly, Dolly touched the rattan with her lips, moving slowly from left to right. Thirteen tender kisses. This was the part she really loved – the chance to show her devotion to the Mistress. She knew that Paulie loved this as well, though not as much as what was coming…

After the thirteenth kiss, Pauline placed the cane behind herself and held it pressed against her own buttocks with a hand clasped at either end of it. Then she opened her legs wide. The classic domina-trix posture.

She looked down scornfully at her Slave.

"Now, you slut: worship at the Altar!"

Dolly looked up at the shaven vagina, put her hands over her own stinging buttocks, then leaned all the way down to kiss the feet of the Mistress, starting with the toes. A special kiss for each toe. After more kisses on each foot, she made her way slowly up along each leg, kissing and sucking and licking and dribbling as she went from one to the other. She continued to grasp her own backside, as per the rules. The legs of the Mistress were so slender, so lean – she loved running her tongue over the long hard muscles, which were just like a young man's. She licked up and down the thighs as she moved towards the Altar.

Pauline moaned and leaned back slightly, looking up to the high ceiling of her studio. She bent her knees a little to open the thighs wider still and give the Slave access to the divine vessel. She gripped the cane harder and pressed it firmly into her own buttocks.

At last Dolly reached the vagina. After a few long licks on either side, over the outer lips of the smooth vulva, she penetrated the cleft and pushed her tongue into the hot wet membranes.

"Ohhh… you lovely slut!" groaned Pauline.

Dolly tasted the fluid, which was as bitter and acrid as always, and pulled out momentarily.

Pauline looked down at her.

"Don't stop, you bitch! Lick that cunt now! All the way!"

Dolly obeyed and pushed her tongue back in. She worked it harder and harder, up and down, round and round, deeper and deeper, and felt Pauline tensing and pushing as she moved towards her climax, moaning loudly. As she finally came with a guttural shout, she pushed her groin hard into the Slave's face and released a surge of acidic come-fluid that made her choke and splutter. Dolly felt the fluid run down her cheeks and into her mouth and her nose but obediently held firm and carried on licking hard. For the ten seconds or so of her orgasm Pauline's thighs clenched and squeezed Dolly's head. Suddenly there was a loud sharp crack from behind her.

Pauline gasped and staggered back. She barely managed to remain standing. She lifted both arms and looked in amazement at the two halves of the broken cane in her hands.

"Fuck! I came so hard I broke the stick!" she exclaimed, still puffing heavily. Then she shook her head and laughed.

Still kneeling, Dolly wiped the pungent fluid from her lips.

"Isn't that bad luck, Paulie?"

"Yes, it is," replied Pauline, ruefully inspecting both bits of wood. "For whom, I wonder?"

# V

## COMING TOGETHER

IT WAS YET ANOTHER hot humid night. Annabel lay naked on her double bed and leafed through her new book. It was unusual for her to be alone at home after midnight on Saturday, but she had so far not replied to Philip's conciliatory letter after they had gone their separate ways at the tennis club. She felt it was better to refrain from replying than to send the wrong reply. In fact she was unsure how to account for her irrational behaviour when the storm had arrived, and even more unsure how to explain the glow of gratification she still felt about the whole episode. She had spent the afternoon in the shops in Charing Cross Road and had come away with a book on Surrealist Art. She realised she was attempting some kind of auto-therapy – trying to understand the urge for disintegration that she knew had always been there inside her, without ever appreciating its overwhelming power. Until now.

She reached for the glass of red wine on her bedside table and took another sip.

As she turned the next page, her telephone rang. It was unusual for anyone to call her this late, so she sat up on the bedside and looked at the phone to check the number. She recognised it at once but waited for her automatic reply to play through and then the response from the caller. She knew it was Dolly.

*"Annabel... Annabel! Are you there? Please answer... please!"*

She picked up the phone.

"Dolly? Is that you?"

*"Annabel! Oh thank God you're there! Please help me!"*

"What's the matter? Where are you?"

*"I've just run away from a party after someone attacked me. I'm in Earls Court Road. Do you live close to here?"*

"Yes – I'm a couple of streets away. Dolly, what's happened to you?"

*"I'm sorry – I'm in a right state. I'm stuck on my own with no money. I don't know how to get home. I don't know what to do… Can I see you? Please?"*

Annabel quickly gave her the address of her flat and put down the phone. She pondered over the coincidence of Dolly ending up late at night so close to her address, and recalled that the girl already knew she lived in Earls Court. But she did sound genuinely desperate on the phone.

Annabel put on a white dressing gown and poured herself some more wine. She went out into her lounge and sat waiting on the settee. She leafed through more pages of her book.

After ten minutes the entry-phone buzzer sounded.

"Are you still on your own, Dolly?"

*"Yes."*

"All right. Come on up".

A few moments later Annabel opened her front door and was dismayed at the sight that greeted her. Dolly was totally dishevelled in a black halter style mini-dress and black fishnet tights which were torn in several places. She stood awkwardly on high-heeled black shoes and looked as if she were about to topple over. Her lip was cut and there was a graze on one knee where the tights had been broken. Her make-up was smudged and running. Her long dark hair was wildly tousled. Worst of all, her eyes were glazed and out of focus. It was obvious she had spent the evening taking drugs.

"Annabel," she murmured, with a strange wide-eyed look. "I'm fucked!"

"Oh Dolly – what a state you're in! Come in, quickly."

Dolly staggered in, dazed by the light in the lounge, as Annabel supported her arm. She led the girl to the settee and sat her on it. Then she knelt down in front of her and took off her high-heeled shoes. Dolly sighed with relief and sank into the comfortable cushions.

"All right," said Annabel, taking her by the hand. "What's happened to you?"

"I've been at a party close to here for the last few hours and I'm stoned out of my head. And a guy has just raped me."

"Oh no…"

"It's not so bad – he fucked me in one of the bedrooms but I managed to push him off before he came. I think some of his spunk shot over me though… Yuk! Here's a bit on my dress…"

"All right. We're going to clean you up, pronto. Come on!"

Dolly was obedient and shame-faced as Annabel took her to the bathroom. She blinked under the bright silver light and seemed bemused by the gleaming white and chrome furniture. Annabel swiftly undid the black dress and Dolly stepped out of it. All she wore now was a battered pair of fishnet tights, which were completely torn away around the backside and the crutch and ripped in several other places.

"Dolly – don't you ever wear knickers?"

"No. Paulie doesn't like me wearing them. She likes me naked underneath."

Annabel sighed and put her arms around Dolly's waist to pull down the tights. The girl moaned as they fell away and left her naked. Crouching down, Annabel was confronted by her shaven vagina, which looked puffy and swollen, but said nothing. Then she saw the purple stripes.

"Dolly – turn round."

She obeyed.

"My God, you're covered with welts and bruises. How long have these been here?"

"A couple of days."

"Did Pauline do this to you?"

Dolly nodded.

"Now I see how she gets those silkscreens." Annabel shook her head. "Don't you object to this kind of treatment?"

"Not really. I'd rather not get hurt but it's all part of my relationship with Paulie, so now it turns me on. I like being told I'm a piece of shit because that's all I've ever been anyway."

"Oh Dolly. What am I going to do with you?"

"You can do whatever you want…" She giggled.

Annabel sighed again and leaned into the shower unit to start the water running. Dolly gazed at the back of her tanned thighs, exposed as the white dressing gown rode up while she operated the shower controls. The shower spurted into life and the water hissed down. As Annabel adjusted the temperature, Dolly saw one of her dangling breasts come partially into view. She loved how clean and strong and healthy Annabel's body looked. Instinctively she fingered her pussy. It was already wet.

Annabel turned round and saw that Dolly was touching herself. She ignored the provocation, reminding herself that the girl was still high on drugs.

"Get in, Dolly. Then we'll do something about those cuts and bruises."

She helped Dolly step into the glass-panelled shower enclosure. The warm water swept over her like a giant caressing hand that made her moan with pleasure. But she was too exhausted to do anything herself. She looked forlornly at Annabel as the water cascaded over her slender body.

"Annabel – will you wash me? Please?"

Suddenly Annabel realised that this was where the new path had led her. As she gazed at the girl, so pale and fragile and beaten, she felt a surge of electricity run through her – as if it was the delayed reaction to the climactic lightning flash of the storm. She couldn't refuse. She had to go to her. She realised now that she had had to from the moment she had seen her standing so submissively beside Pauline at the Reunion Party. Her body had known what she wanted long before the thought had arrived in her head.

Looking hard at Dolly, Annabel slipped off the dressing gown and stepped into the shower. Dolly's mouth dropped and she stared back as Annabel took some bath gel and a sponge. In the confines of the enclosure their bodies were virtually touching. Both were now thoroughly sprayed with warm water.

"Oh God!" Dolly blurted out. "You're so fucking beautiful…"

"Don't say anything," replied Annabel softly. She touched the girl's face with the wet sponge. Dolly shut her eyes and was in rapture. She was close to tears.

Annabel poured gel onto the sponge and carefully proceeded to wash Dolly around the neck, over the shoulders and the chest and the belly, moving in slow circles. She avoided the genitals and sponged over the hips and the buttocks. Then she leaned down to wash the legs, starting with the thighs and moving to the knees; she crouched to do the calves and finally the feet, above and below, including the toes. She was surprised by the emotions this aroused in her. She realised how much she had missed the simple joy of washing and tending to someone younger and smaller and weaker than herself – someone physically dependent on what she did.

She stood up. Finally she had to attend to the place that needed cleaning more than anywhere else. Gently she touched the sponge to the genitals. Dolly moaned and opened her eyes. She put her arms around Annabel's neck and looked straight into her face, only inches away. She smiled joyfully. Annabel began to wash the vagina, parting the lips tenderly to ease the soapy sponge further and further inside. Dolly groaned and laid her forehead against Annabel's, drawing her closer. Their bodies pressed against one another, the water barely finding space to run between them.

Annabel took a deep breath. She couldn't pretend any longer. She put her free hand under Dolly's chin to lift it with one finger and kissed her full on the mouth. Dolly responded and their mouths opened and their tongues met. As their kiss deepened, Dolly sobbed somewhere in her chest. She knew at once that this was the most precious moment of her life. As Annabel continued to wash her, Dolly allowed the sob to flow down through her body like a big shining sea-wave until it reached her genitals, and she came with a sharp twitching spasm and a muffled cry in Annabel's mouth while they were still kissing. Annabel dropped the sponge and took the girl completely into her arms. At this point Dolly reached Heaven and wanted nothing more than to die, there and then, before it was taken away from her.

The Sunday morning sun blazed into the lounge. Dolly gulped down the last of the tea and put the cup on the tiled coffee table. She leaned back into Annabel's comfortable settee and yawned contentedly, stretching her naked body like a cat. She looked admiringly around the beautifully furnished room, replete with books and CDs and DVDs. A large television screen faced her across a sumptuous Persian rug. Tasteful posters and paintings adorned the walls.

Annabel, naked apart from a striped blue apron, walked in from the kitchen.

"Do you feel better now?" she asked.

"Yes. Still a bit hung over but much better. Thanks for the breakfast. I couldn't eat any more."

Annabel sat down beside her. At once Dolly leaned into her and Annabel put her arm around her shoulder.

"Dolly, I think you should stay with me today."

"I'm happy to stay with you for as long as you want. Hold me tighter…"

"Does Pauline know you're here?"

Dolly shook her head.

"What would she say if she knew?"

"She'd probably cane me straight away!"

"Why do you stay with her when she treats you so badly?"

Dolly paused.

"Because – she knows stuff about me that could get me arrested and sent to prison. Drug-dealing, mainly. I did a lot of it when I first came to London, last year, just to survive. She has incriminating evidence that she could give to the police."

"So she's blackmailing you?"

"Yes, I guess you could call it that."

Annabel frowned. She was not the least bit surprised.

"Isn't there anyone who can help you?"

"I don't think so. Everyone's scared of her. She has friends who are criminals and gangsters. She's not the kind of person you want as an enemy. In the last few months she's been taking more and more cocaine and other bad stuff and keeps getting into a temper. One day I think she's going to do something *really* crazy. She can be very violent, you know."

"Yes. I remember her from school. She was regarded as a bit crazy even then. It sounds as if she's become far worse now. How did you come to meet her?"

"At an art college party in Shoreditch. One of my old school friends is a student there."

"Where are you from, Dolly?"

"Oh, some boring run-down place on the south coast. A dead-end town full of closed-down shops. I thought I'd try my luck in London, but it's really tough here on your own. Everyone's trying to fuck you, one way or another."

"Does that include me?"

"Of course not, silly. *I* want to fuck *you*. I wanted to from the moment I saw you." She reached behind Annabel to untie her apron string.

"You're as direct as ever!" said Annabel. To please Dolly, she took off her apron and dropped it on the coffee table. Dolly wolf-whistled. They both laughed. Then Dolly was serious again.

"Paulie's fucked me from day one, and made no bones about it. But she does look after me, and gives me somewhere to live. And she really is an interesting person. It's better being with her than wait-ressing all day long and earning sod all."

"But she makes you pay a big price."

"I have to earn my way."

"How?"

"I have to fuck whoever she tells me to. Any person, any age."

"Does she receive money for that?"

"Yes, sometimes. But I don't know how much. A lot of the time she pimps me out to get favours from people in return."

"It sounds as if she has you as her prisoner."

Dolly smiled, with a look of weary resignation on her face.

"Her prisoner. Her slave. Her whore. Whatever she wants me to be. She knows what a loser I am."

"Don't you want to get away from her?"

Dolly touched Annabel's heavy breast and gently squeezed it.

"Annabel – I'd leave her straight away for you. I'd leave them all for you."

"Oh Dolly, I know how much you want me. But I don't know how far I can take a relationship like this. I've never done this before, with another girl – except once at university."

"Did you enjoy it?" She ran her finger back and forth over Annabel's protuberant nipple.

Annabel paused.

"Yes, I did. But she was older than me."

"How much older?"

"A lot. She was a lecturer at the university. She seduced me."

"Wow! That's so sexy! What was her name?"

Annabel smiled and stroked Dolly's hair.

"That's going to remain a secret."

"All right. So how long did it last?"

"Almost a year. We've remained friends since then. You could say she's my lifelong mentor. We still write to one another, though I haven't seen her for a long time."

Dolly giggled.

"You like shagging your teachers, don't you?"

Annabel removed Dolly's hand from her breast.

"Dolly, what do you know about me and my teachers?"

Dolly gulped.

"I'm sorry, Annabel. But Paulie told me about what happened at St Margaret's."

"I see. When did she tell you about this?"

"After you left the Black Sun Gallery. She was pissed off when you turned her down for the life-casting. She was dead keen to make a model of you."

"How much did she tell you about what happened at school?"

"Everything. About how she blackmailed you after she heard you shagging the Biology teacher. How she made you strip naked and jump from the bridge…"

"What else?"

Dolly paused.

"She said you were so scared up on the bridge that you peed yourself. And then you begged and begged her to save you and cried like a baby until she pulled you out of the river with her hockey stick. The one I gave you at the party. Is all that really true?"

Annabel looked down, obviously embarrassed. She sighed.

"Yes, it's all true. Pauline totally humiliated me. It's haunted me ever since. I don't think I've fully recovered from it, one way or another."

Dolly looked shocked. Annabel smiled at her ruefully.

"I'm sorry if that spoils the image you have of me. As you can see, *I'm* a loser as well."

Dolly shook her head and put her arms around Annabel.

"It doesn't spoil anything. It just makes me want you even more!"

Affectionately, Annabel kissed Dolly's forehead and stroked her hair. She noticed it was dyed dark brown and was actually light red underneath, but decided to say nothing about it.

"My lovely Dolly. I'm beginning to like that name. Even though it isn't your real one. At least, that's what Pauline told me. Is *that* really true?"

"Yes," she replied. "It's true. Dolly is the name Paulie gave me – because I remind her of a favourite doll she had as a child. She won't allow me to use my real name, or even tell anyone what it is, as long as I'm with her."

"Don't you mind losing your name?"

"No. I'm happy to get rid of it, along with all the other crap I've left behind. I can try to be a different person here in London. A better person."

"Even so – I'd love to know who you really are."

Dolly stood up and turned to face Annabel. She moved her legs wide apart and set her knees down on the settee on either side of Annabel's thighs, so that she knelt up facing her at close range, looking down at her. She put her hands on Annabel's shoulders and grinned.

"When I'm not with Paulie any more, I'll tell you my real name. But only if I'm sure you really want me… if you want me to be with you, all the time. Then I'll come clean and tell you everything about myself. Every last shameful bit."

"All right," smiled Annabel. "It's a deal."

Dolly's heart jumped.

"Does that mean you really want me?"

Annabel put her hands on Dolly's hips and squeezed gently. She could see the tips of the purple cane-marks at the side of Dolly's buttocks. This confirmed her reply.

"Yes. I want you to be my Dolly. All the time."

"Oh Annabel!"

Dolly leaned down and they kissed again, for a long time and without pause, Dolly's tongue eagerly licking and probing into every part of Annabel's mouth. Her svelte thighs opened wide as she slowly sank down onto Annabel's chest and lap. As their genitals brushed and then gently rubbed together, Annabel could smell the sweet girlish odour of Dolly's excitement. It was intoxicating. It was like being with a new, younger part of herself, hitherto unknown but now irreplaceable. Annabel felt herself responding, the heavy scent of her own arousal soon mingling with the girl's. She realised that she needed Dolly in her life. In fact she wanted this adoring unruly creature more than anything else she could imagine. Even if the prospect of any long-term relationship was unrealistic, given the many differences between them, she knew she had to do whatever she could to rescue Dolly from her tyrannical Mistress. Even if that meant incurring Pauline's hostility again.

Alone in her studio, Pauline was dressed in rough denim overalls. She was working on a nine-foot length of hefty steel girder and spray-painting it in black gloss, making it look unnaturally smooth and luminous. Another girder, six feet in length, lay waiting for the same treatment. These items were the foundation of her masterpiece, which she had now formulated clearly in her mind.

When she had finished spraying the first girder, Pauline took a break and lit a cigarette. She gazed pensively at the lengths of metal, looking from one to the other, making calculations.

As she reached the end of her cigarette, the telephone rang. As always, Pauline waited to listen to the voice message.

It was Dolly's voice.

*"Paulie, it's me. Sorry I haven't got back today, but I got totally stoned at the party last night and had a fucking rough time. So I stopped off at Annabel's place to get my head together. She's really looked after me well, you know, being a doctor, so I feel a bit better. I'm stopping over with her tonight and I'll be well enough to come home tomorrow, about twelve noon. Sorry I couldn't be there to help you today. Lots of love..."*

Pauline snorted and shook her head. She didn't bother to pick up the phone.

"You little tart," she said, putting out the cigarette. "You went and did it. I knew you would!"

# VI

# APHRODITE

A NNABEL DID OF COURSE have to see Philip again after the episode on the tennis court, and met him in London on the Saturday following the commencement of her affair with Dolly. They went to their favourite Greek restaurant in Covent Garden and then watched a light-hearted play in a nearby theatre before ending the evening in his flat near St Pancras. She freely allowed him to take her in bed as usual, which he did all night long with the ardour of a man who fears that his woman is on the verge of leaving him; but although she enjoyed the physical sensation of his passion, she was unable to achieve any climax herself. For Annabel this was strikingly unusual. She was uncharacteristically subdued and withdrawn throughout the weekend, and unwilling to talk to Philip about her thoughts or her feelings. She knew that the entry of Dolly into her life had brought her to yet another emotional crossroads, and she needed direction from the one person who could provide it.

Annabel's secret lover at university was Professor Dr Miriam Hirsch, who was now in her late fifties and lived alone in semi-retirement in the tranquil suburbs of North Oxford. The two of them had kept up a close and confidential hand-written correspondence ever since their university affair had ended, and whenever Annabel went to visit Miriam in person, on an irregular and infrequent basis, there was invariably a rekindling of their erotic relationship. For this reason Miriam was always happy to welcome Annabel for an overnight stay. Annabel went to see her whenever she felt in need of advice and comfort. The latter included intimate physical pleasure, of a sort that she couldn't obtain from a man. With Miriam she felt closer to her true self than with anyone else she knew.

One Friday afternoon in early August, Annabel drove up to Oxford in her small compact car. She was dressed exactly as Miriam liked, in a crisp white blouse and sensible knee-length black skirt, with black knee-high socks and black shoes, and had her hair pulled back into a long girlish pony-tail. This was the way she had often looked when she had been a student. As always, she brought with her a box of chocolates and a bunch of Miriam's favourite flowers. This was a little odd, as Miriam was without question the masculine, dominant partner in their relationship, as befitted her greater age and intellect, but there was much that was unusual in this long-running liaison. Each woman was of course free to do whatever she wanted with other partners, but both had to confess in full to one another whenever they met. In recent years this had increasingly meant that Annabel confessed a great deal to Miriam, since the latter had had fewer and fewer affairs as she grew older. Annabel enjoyed this immensely, as she could trust her mentor's total discretion, and knew that Miriam was always aroused by hearing her talk about her adventures. In return, Miriam took great pleasure in analysing her young lover and dispensing advice and guidance. It was a kind of therapeutic foreplay, all the more powerful for being serious.

Annabel arrived and parked her car in the straight tree-lined street. She was a little early. She took the flowers and a carrier bag from her car and walked up to the genteel Victorian semi-detached house. Its red-bricked walls looked warm and welcoming in the summer sun. She opened the squeaky wrought iron gate and walked up the path that led to the entrance door, located at the side of the house. The front garden was, as usual, somewhat overgrown. Miriam came round to meet her from the back garden, arms open wide. She was dressed in a loose baggy full length sleeveless white frock, and Annabel could see that she had put on some weight since their last meeting nearly a year ago. She still managed to disguise the effects of her arthritic knees. Her hair was now entirely grey but still cut very short all round, still very smart, and her long bony face and sharp black eyes were as impressive as ever, despite the round-framed pair of glasses she now wore.

"Annabel! Annabel!"

Miriam took the flowers, wedged them in the wooden fence, and embraced Annabel like a long-lost daughter. They hugged with intense emotion. They were roughly the same height, but Miriam was larger and heavier. Annabel was momentarily crushed by the intensity of her embrace.

"Oh my dearest girl, it's been far too long!" exclaimed Miriam.

"Far too long," agreed Annabel. "Forgive me for being away for ages. And then coming to see you only when I need you."

"Don't worry about that," smiled Miriam, briefly kissing her on the lips. "I like you best when you're needy!" Appreciatively, she stroked the sleek dark pony-tail.

She ushered Annabel into her house. The lounge was as cool and spacious as always, and dominated by a large piano, an extravagantly exotic pot plant and several crammed bookcases. The smell of cooking stew came in from the kitchen.

"Any new acquisitions?" asked Annabel, inspecting the antiques and curios which were lined up all over the grand old fireplace.

"Nothing special," replied Miriam. "I'm too busy working these days, even though I've given up teaching. Glass of sherry?"

"Just a small one, please. You said on the phone you were working on a new paper."

"Yes, on latest research into improving stroke rehab procedures. I hope to stretch it out into a full length textbook in due course. I'll do well if it gets published in America."

"I look forward to reading it. I'll stack it next to your other books."

Miriam smiled and handed her a glass of sherry.

"I'll make sure you get a signed copy."

"Miriam, there's the most wonderful aroma coming from your kitchen…"

"I've prepared a lamb casserole for us, to eat later."

"Oh, I can't wait," said Annabel, sampling the sherry.

Miriam sat down on her thickly padded red couch and patted the seat cushion next to her. This was now the ritual procedure. Annabel sat down beside her. Their thighs touched and Miriam immediately put her arm around Annabel's shoulders. She was sympathetic.

"I'm so sorry to hear about Sister Helena."

Annabel sighed.

"Yes, Miss Davis confirmed the diagnosis when I telephoned her. Helena has pancreatic cancer. Inoperable. She probably has a year left, maybe less."

"How old is she?"

"Early sixties. We all thought she'd go on as Headmistress for at least another ten years."

Miriam shook her head.

"I never met her, but I know she was pretty much your second mother."

"I think *you're* my second mother, Miriam. In fact, you're as good as my first mother, since my real one is always too drunk for any worthwhile conversation."

Miriam kissed Annabel's cheek.

"I'd be happy to be your first *and* second mother, if I could see more of you. But I know how busy you are. And how many people there are who demand your time and attention. Are things going well at the hospital?"

Annabel shrugged.

"So-so. As usual, we're being asked to do more and more with fewer and fewer resources…"

"As usual. But you're not here to talk about work."

Annabel looked at the thick carpet at her feet.

"Miriam, I know it sounds dramatic, but I really think I've lost my way. In my personal life."

Miriam held her close and stroked her shoulder.

"I assume that's why you're here, my dearest."

"When I started up with Philip a few months ago, I thought I had it all. A handsome, wealthy, successful man, full of energy and confidence, and terrific in bed. But now I just don't know what to think. The more he desires me, the more he takes me, the more empty and lonely I feel. Does that make sense?"

"It's not uncommon. It simply means he's not really the right man, despite all appearances. Our needs are very subtle and complicated, Annabel."

"I was hoping to find some kind of support or direction when I went to the St Margaret's Reunion at Midsummer. You know, the old School… the old Faith."

"Annabel, you lost your Catholic Faith a long time ago. As I did my Jewish Faith. There's no going back, I'm afraid – however many times you return to the old family."

"This time things have got even more confusing. As I explained to you in my letter…"

An alarm went off in the kitchen.

"You'll have to excuse me," said Miriam. "I need to see to the casserole. We'll talk about this properly later on. Back here in the lounge. Are you ready to eat – out in the kitchen?"

"Oh yes," smiled Annabel. "I can't wait."

For the next hour they dined in Miriam's kitchen, sitting at her heavy oak table, and spoke about professional and academic matters, going over the old days at Oxford. The casserole was as delicious as usual, as was the dessert that followed, and Annabel relaxed after a couple of glasses of wine.

"Miriam, that was a wonderful meal. Thank you so much. Do you want help with the clearing-up?"

Miriam shook her head. "Leave it to me."

She paused, and reached over to squeeze Annabel's hand.

"Do you want to confess to me, Annabel? On the couch?"

"Yes, I want to, very much. That's really why I've come to see you."

"I know it is. Get yourself ready next door and I'll be there in a few minutes."

Annabel smiled gratefully and went back to the lounge. It was growing dark outside and the room was now illuminated only by a tall standing lamp with a warm red shade. She kicked off her shoes, then slowly took off all her clothes and left them scattered at the foot of the couch, in order to demonstrate her daughterly need for guidance, as Miriam always liked her to do. She untied the pony-tail and shook her hair loose. Now naked, she felt free and relaxed, as if she were a child again. Every girl needed a Mother Confessor for her emotional health, and Annabel was no exception. She sat on the couch and for some time gazed appreciatively at the large painting above the fireplace, showing a splendid voluptuous Aphrodite emerging from the sea. Then she swung her legs onto the couch and lay down on her back, taking up the full length of the seating space. She placed a cushion under her head and took a few deep breaths. She listened to the strains of an Elgar song coming from the kitchen, issuing from Miriam's portable CD player while she cleared the dishes from the table. The contralto's voice was exquisite. Annabel closed her eyes and imagined herself on a beach at sunset, naked, walking towards the sea to greet Aphrodite...

After a few minutes Miriam walked in, still dressed in her white frock. She had left her spectacles in the kitchen. She took a chair and sat down by Annabel's prone figure. Her cheeks were a little red, partly from the wine and partly from the sight of her former student's nude body lying in front of her. She took Annabel by the hand and smiled affectionately at her.

"Now, my darling," said Miriam, "let's talk about your letter. You say you've been thrown into confusion by this teenage girl – Dolly?"

"Yes. Total confusion."

"And her companion – that obnoxious girl who did you such a bad turn when you were at school together. Pauline?"

"Yes. Pauline is her lover. And a cruel and tyrannical Mistress."

"Who constantly flogs her?"

"Yes. Regular systematic caning."

"Of course. She takes advantage of Dolly's low self-esteem and perpetually reinforces it. A truly vicious circle. Does Dolly enjoy the punishment?"

"Yes, at least when she's on cocaine. She likes to be made to feel she's just a slave and a whore. Which of course she is, as long as Pauline goes on dominating her."

"And she's actually a prostitute as well?"

"Yes. Pauline farms her out for sexual favours and pays Dolly a small amount in return. And of course she provides her with a home and looks after her. Nobody will harm Dolly as long as they know Pauline is her Mistress."

Miriam nodded.

"A classic case of exploitation and entrapment. It happens to a lot of vulnerable young people, and not just in London. And now of course *you've* come along to shake things up."

"Miriam, I can't stand by and watch her being abused. I have to do something to help her."

"Does she want you to help her?"

"Yes. She wants to be with me, and no-one else."

"What are your feelings for this girl?"

Annabel paused. Then she decided she had to be completely honest.

"I adore her. She's like a younger part of me – so wild, so cheeky, so high-spirited... so emotional. In fact I was never as wild and spontaneous as she is, even when I was a young child. I just feel so happy and so *alive* when I'm with her."

"And her feelings for you?"

"She's very passionate about me, very intense, very sexual. It's an amazing experience, having a young girl come onto me so directly. I still can't quite believe it. She just grabs me and strips me and... takes me like a desperate teenage boy."

"And you like it?"

"Yes, I love it – having her mouth and her hands all over me, everywhere. I can't deny her, whatever she wants to do. I love the feeling that she's *feeding* on me, like... like a hungry lion cub eating raw meat."

"That's hardly surprising. You see yourself as the mother and Dolly as your daughter, the daughter you've always wanted but never had, so it's natural that you'd want to give yourself to her. To feed her with yourself."

"Yes, I realise that."

"And likewise Dolly sees you as the mother she's never had. It's a very powerful emotional connection – for both of you."

"Miriam, I've been aware of that from the start. But it's even more powerful, because what we have between us is very sexual as well. Dolly wants the sex more than I do, but I still love it when we get physical. I've never known anything like it."

"Do you orgasm frequently?"

"Oh yes, a lot. She uses… all kinds of sex toys on me, and she's very skilful with her hands and her tongue. She's been having sex since she was thirteen."

"Your passion for her isn't surprising. You've often confessed to me that you like being the submissive partner in any sexual relationship. As you've always been with me. But it seems to me that you find it easier to be like this with another woman – not with a man."

Annabel looked up at her and nodded.

"You're right. I couldn't submit to a man, not emotionally, although I love the sensation of being physically dominated… being on the bottom, you know, under a man's big hard body. I only want a strong man – when it comes to sex."

"Yes, but you can't submit to a man emotionally, or spiritually, if you want to put it like that. I suspect you have the same problem now with Philip."

Annabel nodded.

"How are things with him?" asked Miriam.

"Not good," replied Annabel. "I spent the night at his flat a couple of weeks ago and he was very passionate, as always. But I couldn't come, however hard he tried. That's when I knew it was over. It's unusual for me not to reach the finishing line."

"Most unusual," smiled Miriam. She paused for a moment.

"And there's no sign of what you've been wanting?"

"No – nothing," said Annabel. "I think the medics are right. It's not going to happen for me, whichever man I'm with." Briefly she shut her eyes.

Miriam gently squeezed her hand.

"Does Philip know about Dolly?"

"No – I can't bring myself to tell him. But he suspects there's someone else."

"It seems to me your relationship with him is over anyway. You've finished with him, as you do with all men. You aren't able to attach yourself permanently to a man."

"It's true. It's always been like that. There's no problem when it's a short affair, but it *does* become a problem when I try to have a long serious relationship with a man. It sounds silly, but it's as if… a man is in *competition* with me."

Miriam nodded.

"That's exactly what it is, my dear. He's in competition with your masculine side. The boyish part of you which likes to win games of tennis and hockey. The part of you that's come down from your father's side. The part that wants to come out on top. It's the part that's made you ambitious and successful. The form captain, the team leader, telling the others what to do!"

Annabel now squeezed Miriam's hand, and looked at her.

"I always thought you liked the boyish side of me."

"I do. It's charming. But only because it's so vulnerable, placed right up against your feminine side, the one that wants to serve, to submit, to love. The part of you that wants to give in. The part you've inherited from your mother."

"I know. There's something deep down inside me that wants to surrender and let everything go, just like *she's* always done. I've come to accept that now."

"And that's the part of you that Dolly has drawn out. Precisely because she's a weak young girl and doesn't challenge your masculine side, you can let loose your feminine side, without inhibition. Clearly it's something you need to do, very badly. That's why you're so strongly attracted to her, and why you love being taken by her. And of course that's why you feel so unsettled by what's happened. Your feminine side, which has always been carefully controlled by your masculine side, is now bursting out, like molten lava pouring out of a volcano."

Annabel's breasts rose and eased sideways as she took a deep breath. She looked up at Miriam. Their hands grasped tightly.

"Miriam, you're right. *You've* always brought out my feminine side, but I've always felt safe giving in to you because you're older than me and understand me. It's different with Dolly, because she's so young and doesn't understand what she's doing. She's all instinct and wild impulse."

"And therefore she's appealing – and dangerous."

"Yes. Not dangerous in herself, but because of the type of people she mixes with and lives with. The type of people I know very little about, with my comfortable background."

"Except for Pauline, of course. The most important of those people."

"Yes. I know all too much about her. I know I'm going to have to confront her at some point if I'm going to make Dolly mine. She won't let her devoted little slave go without a struggle. I know I'm going to have to pay a price of some kind to get Dolly out of her clutches."

"Does that frighten you?"

"Yes, it does frighten me, but it excites me too. I want Dolly to know that I gave everything I had in order to get her. I want her to be aware, always, that I made a big sacrifice for her, to prove to her that she's really worth something. I want that sacrifice to be what keeps us together in the future... what keeps our love alive."

Miriam was amused.

"Still the ardent Christian, then, underneath it all!"

Annabel smiled back wryly.

"Once a Catholic…."

"But do you really see a future with Dolly?"

Annabel sighed.

"I don't know. I'm probably mad to think there could be a future for us. But I know I have to try."

"Do you want to live with her?"

"Yes. I want to look after her and keep her safe and make her happy. And help her make something of her life."

Miriam smiled indulgently at her.

"Do you think I'm a fool, Miriam?"

"Yes, Annabel, you *are* a fool – like everyone else who's fallen in love with the wrong person and can't do a thing about it. There's no greater joy in life, I can assure you."

"Then I'm happy to be a fool."

Miriam brought Annabel's hand to her lips and kissed it tenderly.

"My darling Annabel. Someone like you makes *me* happy – happy to be alive, even though I'll never be the recipient of the kind of love you have for Dolly. I've always regarded you as my very own Aphrodite, and now you've shown me how right I was. I'm so pleased to see you in love with someone at last – and with a girl! – and seeing for yourself just how much distress that causes! I'm truly happy for you – though I'm envious of Dolly as well!"

Annabel ran her middle finger to and fro over Miriam's lips, then put it slowly in her mouth. Miriam sucked it and moaned with pleasure.

"Oh Miriam… I have missed you. I'm sorry it's been so long." She raised and drew aside her knee, the one nearest to Miriam, then opened her legs as wide as the couch permitted to present her genitals to her Mother Confessor. To please her old lover, she had ensured that the dark pubic hair was fully intact, untrimmed, as nature intended.

Miriam took a deep breath. She removed Annabel's finger from her mouth and put her hand on the raised knee. A young woman's knee… so round, so firm, so healthy.

"Will you stay the night?"

"Oh yes, I'd love to stay. All night." Annabel smiled mischievously. "Even though I suspect I won't get much sleep…"

Miriam smiled back, equally mischievous. She moved her hand down from the knee and gently touched Annabel's clitoris with one of her fingers. It was stiff and engorged, and she was already wet.

"I can promise you that you won't get *any* sleep tonight, Annabel!"

Annabel laughed, but she couldn't conceal her excitement. Her eyes shone as she looked up at Miriam. "Do you want me to go upstairs?" she asked in a low voice.

"Oh yes, please do…" Miriam withdrew her hand.

Annabel rose and stood up in front of Miriam, who remained sitting on the chair. She put her hands behind the older woman's head and caressed the cropped grey hair, as Miriam reached behind her and held her warm buttocks. She looked up at her beloved student.

"Annabel, you're as beautiful as the first day I saw you, bathed in sunshine while you sat by the window, waiting for me in my study, for our first tutorial. The moment you smiled at me, as I walked in, I fell in love with you. Straight away! The only time that's ever happened to me! I hope it wasn't too obvious."

"No, it wasn't. What I do remember is how very impressed I was by you – straight away! – and I was so pleased to be in your hands. And I still am…"

She leaned down and planted a long kiss on Miriam's forehead. Then she turned away and walked out of the lounge.

Miriam sighed. She got up from the chair, as her knees were starting to hurt, and turned to face the fireplace. She listened as Annabel carefully ascended the creaky wooden stairs to the bedroom. Naked foot treading softly on aged timber… what a wonderful sound.

She stared for a while at the painting of Aphrodite and her eyes gradually filled with tears. The Goddess of Love had blessed her for one more night and she was grateful.

## VII

## TRUE HEARTS

THE FOLLOWING SUNDAY afternoon Annabel and Dolly sat near the top of the park at Primrose Hill, making the most of the sunny weather and the fresh breeze. They wore light summer frocks with thin shoulder straps, Annabel in pink and Dolly in yellow, and picnicked on small pies, olives and cakes which they had bought from the shops at the foot of the Hill. They looked over the tree tops at the roofs of London Zoo and listened to the distant cries of the exotic birds.

"It's so lovely here," sighed Dolly. "Can't you buy one of those big old houses down there, in that street? Then we could live there together and spend every Sunday sitting up here on top of the hill."

"I wish!" laughed Annabel. "Even a doctor can't afford to buy one of those places. They cost an absolute fortune. I'm afraid we'll have to make do with sitting on the grass."

"All right," replied Dolly. "I don't mind – as long as I can sit with you."

Annabel put an olive between finger and thumb and raised it to Dolly's mouth. The girl saucily conveyed it into her mouth on her tongue.

"Mmm... that tastes nice." She looked out towards the Zoo and grew pensive.

"Annabel... how did it go on Friday with your old tutor in Oxford?"

"It was very pleasant. I hadn't seen her for a long time, so we had a lot of catching up to do. We had lots to talk about."

"Did you stop with her overnight?"

"Yes, I did."

Dolly was characteristically direct.

"Did you sleep with her?"

Annabel was characteristically truthful.

"Yes, I did."

A little apprehensive, Dolly turned to face her.

"Do you mind me asking you about this?"

"No, I don't mind. You're entitled to ask me."

"All right. Did you have sex with her?"

"Yes, we did have sex."

"Did she fuck you?"

"Yes, if you want to put it like that. She's always been the dominant one. That's the way we both like it."

For the first time in her life, Dolly wanted someone badly enough to feel jealous. She ran one of her fingers up and down the underside of Annabel's thigh, which was fully exposed as she sat on the grass with one knee raised up. The firm bronzed leg was moist with perspiration. Suddenly Dolly wanted to make love to her again, more than she had ever wanted to before, and wished that they were back in the flat in Earls Court. She wanted Annabel all the time, like an addictive drug that took away the pain of her emptiness and made her glad to be alive. But she resented sharing her with anyone else. Briskly she waved away a wasp.

"Does she use the sort of toys and gadgets I use on you?"

"No. Only the gadgets that Nature's given her," laughed Annabel.

"Does she satisfy you? Does she make you come?"

"Yes. She always does."

Dolly withdrew her hand and licked Annabel's salty perspiration from her finger. She vowed that she would lick every last drop of sweat from Annabel's body when they returned to her flat later that day. It would take her *ever* such a long time…

"Are you turned on because your Oxford woman is so much older than you?" asked Dolly.

"Yes. That's part of the pleasure. But it's mainly about the kind of person she is."

"Does she love you?"

"Yes. She loves me very much, and has done from the moment we first met. I've had to step back from any full-time relationship with her – really, to be fair on *her*. I'm very fond of her but I can't respond with the same kind of feeling she has for me. She understands that. She's happy to love me part-time."

"Are you going to keep on seeing her?"

Annabel's hair and the skirt of her pink frock fluttered momentarily in the breeze. She looked towards the Zoo and thought carefully before replying.

"Yes, I want to keep on seeing her. She's a big part of my history – you could say she's now become part of *me*. I suppose because she's a woman, I've never put her in the same category as a male lover. I would never want to have a relationship with two men at the same time, but my Oxford lover is something different. I've always kept our affair secret, as she has, so it's never seemed to make any difference to any other relationship I've been in. But whenever there *was* someone I was deeply, passionately involved with, I wouldn't see her during that time."

Dolly tentatively put her hand on Annabel's.

"Are you deeply, passionately involved with me?"

Annabel looked into her eyes and took her hand.

"Yes, my love, I *am* deeply involved with you. And passionately too. Do you want me to stop seeing my old flame? I will stop, if that's what you want."

Dolly clasped Annabel's hand, again marvelling at how warm it was. The heat of her lover's body always made Dolly feel like melting away inside. She looked down at her own bare white feet and felt small and cold and insignificant by comparison.

"Yes. I *do* want you to stop, Annabel. So I can be sure *I'm* the one you really love. And…"

"And what…?"

Dolly swallowed hard.

"And… I want to be the only one who knows what you look like when you come. I want you to come just for me, and nobody else."

Annabel smiled, charmed by her jealousy, and aroused by what she had just said. She took great pleasure from Dolly's unquenchable desire for her, but was careful not to take advantage of it. She stroked the girl's hair, moving it away from her face so she could see her properly. Gently she ran her finger over the freckled nose.

"Do you want me to stop seeing everyone else?"

Embarrassed, Dolly nodded, still staring at the grass. She felt like a mean little child.

"All right, Dolly. I *will* stop. For you."

Dolly looked back up at Annabel.

"What about your boyfriend – Philip?"

"I've already stopped seeing him, in any way that matters. But it's difficult to tell him why. I want to be sure about you and me before I explain things to him. He'll think I've gone crazy."

Dolly ran her other hand up along Annabel's bare arm. She couldn't hold back what she felt.

"Annabel, I've never been so sure about *anything* as I am about you. I've never met anyone like you before, and I know I never will again. You're the only thing that makes my life worth living!"

"Oh Dolly, please don't say that. You have so much to live for." She stroked her hair again.

Embarrassed by her moment of weakness, Dolly abruptly leaned over and kissed Annabel on her lips.

"Yum-yum!" she exclaimed, trying to lift her own spirits. "You taste of peppered olives!"

They both laughed. Then Dolly grew serious again and looked back at her feet.

"I can't ask you to be faithful to me while I'm fucking every so-and-so that Pauline tells me to. It's not fair on you."

Annabel squeezed her pale hand.

"My darling, I've never been the jealous type. Love can't always run in a straight line. I know you can't help the situation you're in, and I know you desperately want to get out of it. All I want you to do is promise me that you'll look after yourself, as well as you can… and promise that you'll come to me in the end, when you're finally free."

"I promise! Absolutely! I want to be all yours, Annabel! More than anything in the world!"

"That's good enough for me, my love."

Dolly put her arms around her and laid her head against Annabel's chest. It always reassured her to listen to her lover's heart beating. For a while they held each other fondly, ignoring the glances from passers-by on the tarmac footpath. Then Annabel looked down and ran her finger along Dolly's exposed back. She was curious about the three-inch tattoo of a winged black dragon, elaborately drawn, located precisely between her shoulder-blades.

"I've noticed this before. It's a very nice piece of work… but it looks rather sinister. Did Pauline give it to you?"

"Yes," replied Dolly. "She got it done for me. It's her way of making a link between me and her artistic demon. It shows I'm connected to her magical force. It shows I belong to her."

"Do you belong to her?"

Dolly shook her head, vigorously. She pulled away and took a small velvet pouch from her handbag.

"I've got something for you. I bought it yesterday, from the Market in Spitalfields."

Annabel watched as Dolly extracted two identical rings from the pouch. They were thin brass trinkets, each with a jade stone set in a small heart-shaped frame at the top.

"I'm sorry they're so cheap, but I can't afford proper jewellery."

"It doesn't matter. I'm not bothered about jewellery anyway. What are they for?"

"For both of us. One for you, and one for me."

Dolly held up both rings, one in each hand.

"I know it sounds silly, but please don't laugh at me. I want us to get… engaged. Secretly. No-one else needs to know. Just the two of us."

Annabel raised her eyebrows in surprise.

"Engaged? You mean, as in engaged to be married?"

"No, not married, but engaged to be true to each other. If we wear the same ring, it'll feel like we… *belong* to each other, always and forever. And then it won't matter what happens to either of us in the short term. We'll always be there for each other in the end."

"Surely it's too early for us to make a commitment like that?"

Dolly looked at her anxiously.

"I know it's too early. But you're the only thing in my life I can hold onto. I need to know you'll always be there for me. Then I can put up with anything that other people do to me."

Annabel realised that this was very important for Dolly and therefore she had to agree. In fact she was touched by the gesture, and by the depth of emotion that lay behind it. Suddenly she felt herself becoming excited by the proposal and what it implied, however foolish and precipitate it might be. The rash young girl inside her once again leapt up towards Dolly. *She* wanted to be a reckless roller-skater as well, hurtling towards the unknown.

"Dolly, it's a *lovely* idea. I accept your proposal."

Dolly beamed with delight.

"But how do we get engaged when we're both girls?" asked Annabel.

"It doesn't matter about that. We just do the same thing, both ways. We swear love and loyalty to each other."

"All right. Who goes first?"

"I'll ask you first. Hold up your left hand."

Annabel did as instructed. Dolly cleared her throat and held up the slightly larger of the two rings. She had rehearsed her lines.

"Annabel… do you swear to dedicate yourself to Dolly, and to Dolly alone… and swear to love her, and cherish her, and protect her – always and forever?"

"Yes, I do. I dedicate myself to Dolly, and swear to love, cherish and protect her."

"And do you swear to do whatever it takes to rescue Dolly from her trap, so she can become a free and happy girl?"

"Yes. I swear to do whatever it takes to rescue Dolly."

"So will you be mine?"

"Yes, I'll be yours. Always."

Dolly slid the ring down onto Annabel's ring finger. It was a perfect fit. They kissed briefly.

"Now it's your turn," said Dolly. She gave the other ring to Annabel and eagerly held up her left hand.

Annabel raised the ring and thought for a moment.

"Dolly… do you swear to love Annabel, truly and honestly, with all your heart?"

"Yes – I swear to love Annabel, with all my heart!"

"Will you be mine?"

"Yes. I'll be yours for as long as the world lasts... for as long as there are stars in the sky!"

Annabel was moved by Dolly's desperate intensity. She slipped the ring onto the girl's finger.

Then each held her left hand up against the other's, so that the rings touched.

"Now we're engaged!" proclaimed Dolly. "We belong to each other. Always and forever!"

"Always and forever!" replied Annabel.

They kissed again, this time with a long and passionate embrace that finally took them all the way down to the grass, lying tightly folded in one another's arms, their mouths pressed firmly together. Many of the passers-by looked at them with amusement and bewilderment. But they were like a pair of infatuated schoolgirls, oblivious to the outside world.

# VIII

# TYPHON

IT WAS THE NIGHT of the Full Moon, early in August. Pauline's white-walled studio once again swirled with sweetly aromatic incense. Black candles burned on tall wrought-iron stands on either side of the six-foot high silkscreen of the ferocious black dragon, mounted on a metal frame at one end of the capacious room. Illumination was provided by silver lighting high up in each corner of the studio. Seven black-robed hooded figures surrounded a large wooden table, covered with a black velvet cloth, on which Dolly lay spread-eagled, naked and motionless, staring at the ceiling with wide glazed eyes. She had been injected with heroin, in addition to the customary cocaine, specially for the occasion. Her wrists and ankles were secured with metal cuffs and chains to the legs of the broad table.

The ritual was about to reach its climax. One of the hooded figures spoke with a male voice:

> *The Primeval Serpent,*
> *The Great Dragon,*
> *Who was and who is,*
> *And who lives through the*
> *Aeon of Aeons:*
> *He is with your Spirit!*

Another figure, again male, provided the Greek translation, speaking in a deeper voice.

> *To Arxegono Fidi*
> *To Megalo Drako*
> *O Opoios eitan kai*
> *O Opoios enai*
> *O Aionas ton Aionon*
> *Einai me ton pneuma sou!*

Yet another figure, the tallest person in the room, the Priestess, stepped forward to the foot of the altar and held up a black cockerel, which had been drugged into silent submission. The long white bony hand, the right, displayed a large black-stoned silver ring on its middle finger, and was clearly that of a woman. The chicken was suspended over Dolly's body while the hooded figure's left hand produced a small ceremonial knife and swiftly, expertly cut its throat. The bird twitched for a few moments as blood squirted and sprinkled all over Dolly's pale body, which remained totally immobile. The Priestess proceeded to move the chicken in circles all over the altar, to ensure that the naked body was covered everywhere with blood. Some of it splashed over Dolly's face, but still she stared blankly at the ceiling.

After exhausting the considerable amount of blood produced by the sacrifice, the Priestess dropped the dead bird into a bowl under the table, by her feet. Then she spoke, loudly, raising her arms to the silkscreen of the dragon.

"O mighty Typhon, King of Death and Lord of Life, accept this sacrifice from your devoted Priestess, and grant all of your Children your limitless Infernal Power, always and forever!"

The others in the room held up their arms and shouted in unison.

"Hail Typhon, King of Death and Lord of Life! Always and forever!"

One of the figures passed a black phallic-shaped dildo, almost a foot long, to the Priestess. She raised it aloft to the Dragon, and continued her invocation.

"O mighty Typhon, Lord of Lust, I offer you the tribute of this Whore of Earth!"

"Hail Typhon, Lord of Lust!" shouted the others.

The Priestess then lowered the dildo and with both hands inserted it slowly into Dolly's shaved vagina, which lay only a couple of feet in front of her owing to the wide angle of the outspread legs. Dolly moaned as the bulbous snake-shaped head and then the thick shaft slid into her body. The Priestess proceeded to masturbate her with practised skill, moving the dildo in and out and round and round with full appreciation of the girl's needs and responses. Dolly started twitching and thrusting with eager passion, mouth open, eyes staring wildly, the gobbets of chicken's blood running over her in darting lines in all directions. Her thigh muscles swelled and hardened as she vigorously pushed herself onto the phallus. She groaned loudly. The chains chafed and ground on the velvet cloth as she strained helplessly against the cuffs. The celebrants continued to shout "Hail Typhon!" as the dildo drove relentlessly in and out, deeper and deeper, well over half-way in, until after some five minutes Dolly abruptly arched her back and climaxed with a long high-pitched scream, mouth gaping and eyes bulging, her vagina clutching the dildo with repeated jerking spasms until she gasped with exhaustion and collapsed back onto the altar. The Priestess held the black shaft deep inside her for at least another minute while Dolly carried on breathing heavily and staring without focus at the ceiling, an expression of almost insane ecstasy on her face. Every few seconds one or the other of her thigh muscles twitched, making the entire leg jerk involuntarily.

Satisfied with the orgasm, the Priestess withdrew the dildo, which was heavily soaked with vaginal fluid, and held it aloft to the image of Typhon. Beside her another celebrant held up a large gleaming silver chalice filled with dark red liquid. The Priestess turned and slowly eased the dildo down some six inches into the chalice, blending the vaginal fluid with the red liquid. She held it there for several moments.

"Thus do I consecrate the Infernal Grail!" she intoned. The others hissed in acknowledgement of the successful consecration.

Finally the Priestess laid the dildo down on the altar, between Dolly's outstretched legs, and took the chalice. She held it up to the image of Typhon.

"I consume the Power of Earth, to make myself a worthy receptacle of your Infernal Force, O mighty Typhon! *To Megalo Drako!*"

She drank deep from the chalice.

Then the Grail was passed from celebrant to celebrant, each one drinking and subsequently shouting "*To Megalo Drako!*"

After this was completed, all present formed a circle around the altar and rubbed their hands gleefully over Dolly's supine body, gathering up as much of the spilt chicken blood from it as they could. She moaned with joy at the feel of so many hands simultaneously pressing and squeezing and rubbing her flesh.

At the Priestess's signal, the celebrants stopped. They smeared their hands thoroughly over their faces, groaning with gratification at the smell of the blood. Finally they turned to face the silkscreen and raised their arms aloft to the Great Dragon.

"The Blood is the Life! Thus do your Children adore you, O mighty Typhon!" shouted the Priestess. "Fill us with your Infernal Power! Always and forever!"

"The Blood is the Life! Always and forever!" responded the others.

"Always and forever..." murmured Dolly, deliriously. Thrilled by the warm throbbing glow between her thighs, and indeed throughout the whole of her body, she rolled her head to one side and slipped away into a deep sleep. She had no idea when or where she would wake up.

## IX

## FINAL PARTING

Philip glanced at his watch again. Twenty minutes late. No message on his mobile phone. This was typical of the way she'd been behaving since the bizarre episode on the tennis court. Of all the women he'd known, Annabel was the most rational, reliable and considerate. But despite spending the night with him three weeks ago, she wouldn't explain her strange behaviour or her withdrawn mood, and in the end had told him that she needed more time to think about their future together. He hadn't heard from her since. It all pointed to one thing: she was involved with someone else. Now it was time to get to the truth.

He wiped his brow to remove the perspiration. The middle of August was often the most humid part of the year, and this evening was no exception. The Greek restaurant in Covent Garden was doing its best to relieve the heat with overhead fans, but the place was still uncomfortable. He sat in his white shirt, his jacket draped over the back of his chair. He tapped his fingers on the wallet file that lay on the white tablecloth in front of him. He summoned the waiter and asked for more mineral water.

Finally, at twenty-five minutes past, Annabel arrived, floating towards him like a vision from a Pre-Raphaelite painting. She wore a diaphanous white full-length frock with slender shoulder straps and an elaborate drawstring around the waist. He groaned inside. She had never looked more enchanting. It was going to make this conversation all the more difficult.

"Phil! So sorry I'm late, my darling!" She kissed him briefly on the lips and sat down opposite him at the small table.

"Not to worry, my love. How are you keeping?"

"Pretty well. Trying to fend off the heat. Things are as crazy as usual at the hospital. And you?"

"Fine, fine. Keeping busy. Nothing amiss. Glass of the usual?"

"Yes, thanks, I'll have a glass of red," she smiled, putting her handbag on the floor near her feet. Her breasts hung bra-less and slightly transparent in the gauzy dress. Her tanned skin glistened but nonetheless she smelled of something sweet and fragrant that matched her appearance. Philip cleared his throat.

"I've been worried about you, Bella, after not hearing from you over the last few weeks."

"Phil, I'm sorry I've been out of touch so long. But there's no need to worry about me. You know, I'm just going through one of those difficult phases…"

Philip went straight to the point, as he had intended.

"Bella, please be honest with me. You haven't spoken to me for the last three weeks. Are you seeing someone else?"

Annabel twirled the thin brass ring on her finger and sighed. Then she nodded slowly.

"Yes, Phil, I am. But it's not quite what you think. It's very… complicated."

"Is it another man or a woman?"

She looked surprised.

"Why do you ask?"

"I'll tell you in a moment. But please answer my question first."

"It's a woman. A young woman. Do you think that's wrong?"

He laughed, somewhat derisively.

"No, not in principle. I'm not surprised to learn that you're bi-sexual, after what I've seen and heard over the last few weeks. But I *do* think it's wrong if you've chucked *me* for a woman!"

The waiter arrived and put the menus on the table. Philip ordered a bottle of wine.

Annabel continued.

"It's not as clear-cut as you think, Phil. Relationships don't always follow simple rules. I've suddenly woken up to something I need now, which I haven't needed before. Sometimes you can't explain these things logically. I'm sorry, because I absolutely don't want to hurt you, but I have to follow where my heart leads me."

"And where is it leading you?"

"Phil – I know we've been together for a while, and I don't want to be dishonest with you, but please don't interrogate me. I'll explain everything to you in due course."

He put his hand on hers.

"Bella – I'm missing you like crazy. You must know that."

She held his hand and smiled regretfully.

"I do know that. But sometimes… sometimes we feel strange things that we can't explain. Things that go back to the earliest parts of our lives and then return to grab us later on."

"Things that go back to St Margaret's School, perhaps?"

She nodded.

"Yes, in some cases all the way back to there."

"Like Pauline Barrie, for example? Or should I say Pauline Potter?"

She let go his hand.

"Yes, like Pauline."

"I know you have some kind of history with her. I'm disappointed that you haven't got round to telling me about it, ever since that morning we were out on the bridge in the woods."

146

Annabel looked down at the table.

"I've been trying to keep my distance from Pauline. She's a bad memory. I would never call her a friend."

"I suppose not. Unlike the St Trinian's girl you met at the Party."

She looked up at him sharply.

"What do you know about the St Trinian's girl?"

"I know that her name is Dolly and you've been seeing a lot of her lately."

Annabel looked sternly at him.

"How do you know I've been seeing her?"

Philip paused as the waiter arrived and poured two glasses of wine. Then he took a deep breath.

"Bella, I have to put my cards on the table. After what I picked up during our trip to St Margaret's, and then your strange behaviour at the tennis court, I made a few enquiries about Pauline Barrie. I was so concerned about what I learned that I hired a private investigator to do some... research for me."

Her tawny eyes flashed.

"You mean you hired someone to follow me around. To spy on me!"

It was his turn to look down at the table. Now he had to come out with what he knew.

"Bella, do you know what kind of girl you're having an affair with?"

Her eyebrows rose sharply. She grinned sardonically.

"Pray tell me about my affair! It seems you know all about it!"

"There's no point in your denying it. My researcher has seen you holding hands with this girl – Dolly – at various places over the last few weeks. Camden Market, the National Gallery... picnicking by Regent's Park, going to numerous restaurants. You've certainly spent a lot of time with her – since you dropped me."

"So I'm holding hands with her. What a scandal!"

Philip sipped at his wine.

"You've been canoodling with her too. Really close-up intimate stuff. Let's be honest, you're hardly platonic friends. She's been seen with her hands on some very… delicate parts of your anatomy, on many occasions. And it's obvious that you're happy about it."

"This is what your investigator has been telling you?"

"Not just telling me. He has photos as well. That's part of his job." He tapped the file on the table.

"Well, I hope you've been enjoying his photos!"

Philip knew Annabel was headstrong but had never seen her get angry before. She was a more formidable adversary than he had realised.

"Bella – this has nothing to do with my enjoyment. Do you know what kind of company your little Dolly keeps? My man has been following *her* as well. In fact, he's spent a lot more time on her than on you."

Her eyes blazed.

"Do enlighten me!"

"She's in deep with the worst people you can imagine. Prostitutes, pimps, drug-dealers, gangsters. I have the details here in this file, but you can take my word for it. My researcher knows his job."

"I'm sure he does…"

"Bella – this girl is going to destroy you if you carry on with her. She's just a kid, for heaven's sake. You can't even be sure how old she is! Please see reason!"

"Philip, do you think I'm an idiot? Do you think I don't know about her background and her circumstances? Hasn't it occurred to you that I'm actually trying to extricate her from her present way of life and help her make something better of herself?"

"But why? Why rescue *her*? There are countless girls in the same boat."

Annabel's chest rose as she took a deep breath.

"Because I'm in love with her! What other reason do I need?"

He put his hand over his face and groaned.

"Oh Christ. You really are in trouble."

"Phil, you don't know what you're talking about. You're being fed lots of spicy information by your private dick, who's just trying to make as much money out of you as he can. That's how he makes his living!"

She gulped down some wine. Philip tried a different tack.

"I've also found out a few things about your old school mate, Pauline."

Annabel looked at him intently.

"And?"

"She's a lot more discreet and reclusive than the St Trinian's girl, but my man discovered that she's been scratching around in London for quite a few years. Before she became an established artist, she made her living as a dominatrix. Apparently quite a sadistic one as well – she'd do the extreme stuff that the other ladies wouldn't. She's a long-standing drug addict. And as if that wasn't enough, she's rumoured to be some kind of witch or black magic cultist. Needless to say, she has the same involvement with seedy underworld types that Dolly does."

"Of course she does! It's Pauline who introduced Dolly to all those people. I'm the one who's trying to take her away from all that!"

Philip shook his head.

"You can't take on someone like Pauline Barrie, with the kind of friends she has. You don't stand a chance against her."

"Maybe not. But I'm going to try, all the same. I have to do whatever I can for Dolly."

He grew agitated.

"Bella, you're way out of your depth here! Please believe me!"

She put her glass down hard.

"Phil, what I believe is that you're a jealous and possessive man who can't let go of me. Like so many others I've known. I'm flattered, but I'm also fed up with it. I'm entitled to make my own choices in life, just as you are…"

"Annabel, I'm trying to help you…"

"No, Phil, you're trying to help yourself. To turn me into a trophy wife who'll provide you with trophy children. Well, it's too late for that now. Much too late!"

She gathered her handbag and stood up.

"Bella – please be reasonable!"

"I've been reasonable for too long already."

"Please sit down…"

She glared at him.

"Don't you *dare* send someone to spy on me again! Or on Dolly! *Ever!*"

She picked up her glass and contemptuously flicked the red wine over the file on the table. Some of it splashed up onto the front of Philip's white shirt. He hissed with annoyance.

"Bugger!"

"We're finished, Phil! I can't trust you anymore! Don't ever speak to me again!"

She stormed off past the astonished waiter, who was just approaching to take their order.

Philip ruefully inspected the spots of red on his shirt, then looked round at Annabel as she walked out of the restaurant.

"You fool," he muttered, shaking his head. "You poor bloody fool!"

At home the next morning, Annabel opened a hand-written letter from Sister Helena and read it while she drank coffee.

*My Dearest Annabel*
*Thank you for your kind letter last week.*
*In reply to your query, I am keeping as well as can be expected at the moment, and I hope to be able to start the new academic year in September. However, my doctor has advised me to retire from my post at the earliest opportunity in order to conserve as much strength as possible, so it's unlikely I shall be able to carry on at St Margaret's beyond Christmas. I have a tumour of the pancreas which is inoperable, and as I explained to you at the Reunion Party, I cannot realistically expect to go on for more than another year. However, I shall depart this world with a happy heart. I couldn't imagine a more fulfilling life than the one I've had at St Margaret's, nurturing and guiding so many talented young women through the most important years of their lives. It's been a wonderful time, and it's the girls like you who have made all the hard work worthwhile.*

*I'm sorry to hear that your relationship with the charming young man I met at the Party hasn't blossomed into a more permanent union, but sometimes these things are beyond our control, even with the best will in the world. In recent years I have come to believe more and more that everything in our lives is fated. You may call it God's Will if you wish, and I know this notion still means something to you, even though you are no longer a formal Believer in our Faith. My feeling has always been that you, Annabel, are fated for something greater than a conventional career and family, even though you have done so very well in your chosen field of work – as I always knew a girl of your exceptional ability would. Throughout your years at St Margaret's I saw at first hand just how generous, selfless and devoted a soul you truly are, and I have always believed that you are destined to be a shining moral and spiritual example to others.*

*In reply to your question about self-sacrifice, it is in my view always commendable for a St Margaret's girl to follow the example of our Saviour and put herself in peril to rescue another, less fortunate soul from wickedness and oppression, especially when that person is as young and vulnerable as the one you describe in your letter. If you are sure that there is no alternative in this situation but to risk your own welfare for this child's, or even to put yourself in danger, then my advice is that you should do so. Be the Good Shepherd who rescues the errant Lamb from the mouth of the Lion, and act without fear or hesitation. It seems to me that you would never be able to forgive yourself if you failed to save this poor girl from the evil forces that beset her. In any event I suspect that you have already made up your mind about what to do, and nothing I say now will stop you.*

*I pray that you will come through your ordeal and at the end of it be a more happy and fulfilled woman, imbued with the Grace of God and the Divine Glory of Our Saviour.*

> *With Love and Blessings*
> *Helena*

# X

## THE PRICE

A S SHE ENTERED Soho, Annabel cagily put on her dark glasses. She realised this was a somewhat melodramatic gesture, but she was in a melodramatic frame of mind. She felt that she was playing a lead part in a scenario scripted by someone else – namely, Pauline – and that she was therefore under surveillance. She was prepared for the part, very glamorous in a pale orange summer dress, sleeveless and backless in recognition of the hot weather, which had continued all the way through to the second half of August. The tight plunging V-neck and narrow waist flaunted her breasts, and the short hem revealed almost all of her brown legs. She walked on tasselled rust-coloured high-heeled sandals. Her dark hair had been re-curled and highlighted with chestnut the previous day. She was determined to be the star attraction on Pauline's turf, which was a smart and well-known social club in the heart of Soho. She was a little surprised at her own vanity. But glamour was a woman's resource when there was something to contest, something to fight for. That something was Dolly.

Annabel checked the contents of her leather handbag. The bulging white envelope was still securely sealed. She walked on, casually glancing at the windows of the restaurants and the porn shops on her route, all busy in the weekday afternoon. She turned into a side street and arrived at the rather anonymous building. The club was housed in a large refurbished eighteenth-century townhouse. She rang the bell at the entrance and gave Pauline's name; the door buzzed and she pushed her way in, removing her dark glasses. A heavily made-up young female receptionist checked her in while a tall male security guard examined the contents of her handbag. As he touched the envelope he looked at her quizzically for a moment and at once she began to feel the worry-worm at work. The guard was clearly unhappy but had to leave the item where it was. Carrying money in an envelope was not a valid security concern, but it did raise the suspicion of drug-dealing. The receptionist directed her to the top floor of the club, and as Annabel climbed the steep narrow flight of old wooden stairs, she was aware of the guard staring up intently at her ascending legs. She suspected he was more interested in looking inside her envelope than up her dress, and for this reason felt doubly uneasy. As she turned to the next flight of steps, she heard him talking into his mobile phone, probably to alert his colleagues. Bad start. She was in trouble already.

The top floor was several flights higher, and by the time Annabel arrived there she was hot and perspiring. As she advanced into the large lounge area, plush in a cosy old-fashioned way, she saw Pauline sitting comfortably in one of a group of heavy old armchairs, a glass of wine on a low table in front of her. She looked very much at ease in a sleeveless mid-length light blue dress, which blended well with her long mane of red hair. Her long white legs were crossed. Annabel was more interested in her two companions, who were standing beside her and talking intently. One was the burly young black man who had greeted her at the entrance of the Black Sun Gallery; the other was a small and distinctly roguish older man, with grey hair, hard narrow eyes and a sharply cut beard, who dominated the conversation. Both men wore snappy suits. When Pauline spotted Annabel, she waved at her to join them.

"Annabel – come over, darling, and say hello to my friends! You've met Sebastian before at the Gallery – and I'd like you to meet Bernie, a very dear pal of mine for many years."

The young man nodded politely, and Bernie stepped forward to shake her hand with an extravagant smile. There was a huge gold ring on his middle finger. He eyed her up and down. Annabel immediately suspected that he was a gangster. Probably in his mid-sixties.

"My goodness! Pauline told me you were attractive, Annabel, but she undersold you big time! What a *pleasure* to meet you!" He spoke with a slightly odd East London accent.

Annabel flashed her most charming smile, shook hands, and sat down on the armchair next to Pauline. She kept her legs tightly closed, and realised that her dress was too short for the occasion. She hadn't expected intrusive male company or deep armchairs. Bernie was openly staring at her with a big smile fixed on his face. His white teeth looked like expensive implants.

"Bernie's in the jewellery business," said Pauline, "and has also bought a number of my art-works. He purchased three of the paintings you saw at the Gallery a few weeks ago."

"Oh – which ones?" asked Annabel.

"The silkscreens. You know, the Lovelines series."

"Yes, I remember those," said Annabel. She wasn't surprised to learn of Bernie's taste in art. He was gazing down at her thighs, after standing in a position directly opposite her. She crossed her legs.

"Bernie does of course know the model," went on Pauline, slyly provoking him.

Bernie grinned at her.

"Young Dolly. What a pretty little thing she is! I've got to know her very well over the past few months. You know, Sebastian and I took her out to the races last weekend. She won a stack of dosh – with a little help from us, of course. Then she blew it all at the casino afterwards. Shame. She had too much to drink and, shall we say, lost the plot towards the end of the evening. Never mind. Easy come, easy go!" He laughed and drank from his wine-glass.

For Dolly's sake, Annabel carried on smiling her most charming smile.

"Annabel," went on Bernie, "would you be interested in joining us one time at the races? It's great fun. We'll supply the cash for the bets…"

"Thank you for the offer, Bernie, but I'm just so busy in my work it's unlikely I'd find the time."

"Oh yes. Pauline tells me you're a doctor – in a hospital."

"That's right."

"Very worthy work. Noble job. Needs great dedication. I *do* admire you, Annabel."

Pauline had got the attention of a waiter.

"Glass of red wine, Annabel?"

"Yes, thanks."

Bernie leaned over to shake her hand again.

"Annabel, I must be leaving now, but let me say what a great pleasure it is to have met you. If you ever change your mind about the races, or fancy your chances at the casino, just let me know. I can *guarantee* you'll win."

"Really? How?"

Bernie grinned.

"Because I own the bloody place!" Sebastian and Pauline chuckled at his cheerful crassness. Annabel forced herself to keep smiling.

"Maybe you can take Annabel and Dolly out on the same trip," said Pauline. "They're very close friends, you know."

Bernie and Sebastian looked at each other.

"Oh my *goodness*, what a bloody brilliant idea!" exclaimed Bernie. "A foursome! Now that would really be something! What a party we could have!"

"Something to think about, for the future" said Pauline, looking mischievously at Annabel.

Bernie noisily drained his glass of wine and nodded.

"You bet, darling! Maybe you can sort something out for us…"

Pauline smiled broadly and raised one of her copper-red eyebrows.

"I'll let you know, darling!"

The two men left, talking excitedly. Bernie gave Annabel one last backward glance.

The waiter arrived with the wine. Annabel relaxed slightly and uncrossed her legs.

"I see that Dolly keeps high-class company."

"These days, Annabel, money is the only class that matters. Bernie has plenty of it. And he's very good fun. Dolly's always happy to go out with him, often for the whole weekend."

Annabel knew that she was being provoked – that the whole scene had probably been set up to make an impression on her. She knew Pauline was taking advantage of meeting on her home turf and was trying to intimidate her. But she had no choice but to play her game.

"How much does Bernie pay to have Dolly for the weekend?"

"Annabel – you know that's a question I can't answer. The real question is: how much are *you* prepared to pay to have Dolly for the weekend? Up to now I've turned a blind eye to your affair and asked for nothing."

"I'm willing to pay your price. The amount we agreed on the phone."

"Do you have the money with you?"

Annabel reached into her handbag. She gave the thick white envelope to Pauline, who put it straight into her own bag at the side of her armchair. She leaned back and smiled triumphantly.

"How about that, Annabel? My upright Form Captain – the Golden Girl of St Margaret's Convent School – is paying me to hire a teenage prostitute! Isn't that delicious?"

Annabel forced herself to stay calm. She had expected a response of this kind.

"I'm not paying for Dolly – she would willingly spend the weekend with me, any time, without asking for a penny. I'm paying for you. For the hold you have over her."

Pauline nodded.

"Fair point. But Dolly is a natural born whore. She always sells herself to the highest bidder. And to anyone who'll give her a line of coke or an Ecstasy tablet – or anything to get her high."

"She doesn't need drugs when she's with me. And she isn't a whore when she's with me."

"You mean true love conquers all?" Pauline was openly contemptuous.

"In our case, yes."

Pauline raised her eyebrows, with obvious irony.

"Well, you could be right. Dolly is certainly in love with you, big-time. I've never known her get so crazy about anyone before. She talks about you non-stop."

"And it seems you've talked freely about me. About what happened between us at school."

"Yes." Pauline became serious. "I think it's right that Dolly does know, otherwise she wouldn't understand the special… connection there is between us."

"As you wish. I have no objection to her knowing."

"She got very turned on, you know – when I told her the story. She wanted to know *all* the intimate details. I think she now feels that you're kindred spirits underneath, despite the outward differences."

Annabel smiled wryly.

"Both victims of Pauline, you mean?"

"Yes – you're both my victims! Isn't that wonderful?"

Annabel swallowed some wine. It helped subdue her anguish. She responded defiantly.

"I'm not used to being a victim, Pauline. It doesn't sit easily with me."

"Is that so? Well, I know you're a brave girl. But bravery won't win this particular game."

"I realise that. As always, it's money that wins. And that's what I'm here to talk about."

"Go on..."

"I'm paying you this amount as a gesture of goodwill. But I don't want to be in a position where I have to do this every time I want to see Dolly."

"Can't you afford the price?"

"You know I can afford it. I'm in a very well-paid job. But that's not the point. I don't want to be just another one of Dolly's customers – competing with types like Bernie for her favours."

"So what do you suggest?"

Annabel paused and took another sip of wine.

"I want to buy Dolly from you, once and for all. I want her for myself – for keeps."

Pauline looked away and whistled under her breath.

"Now *that* would have to be a *very* big payment, Annabel!"

"I know. Are you prepared to consider it?"

"I'm prepared to consider anything. But I've never thought of… actually valuing Dolly as a capital asset. What a thought! It's like selling a slave to another merchant – just like they did in ancient Rome!"

"I'm not a slave merchant. I'm buying Dolly's freedom."

Pauline gulped down her wine. She was clearly excited by the proposition, and rather amused. She looked hard at the carpet, then back at Annabel.

"You know that Dolly owes me a lot of money?"

"Yes. She told me that you bailed her out when she got into debt with a drug dealer."

"Did she tell you how much?"

"Yes. It was a very large amount. But it doesn't matter. I'm willing to cancel her debt."

Pauline shook her head, sardonically.

"You must have it really bad, darling, to make an offer like this. You must be seriously in love with the girl."

"I am in love with her. I want her to live with me, full-time, and I want to look after her. There's no point in pretending otherwise."

"And you're prepared to pay… many thousands of pounds for that?"

"Yes."

"But what if Dolly just… ups and leaves you, after you've paid a fortune for her? After all, she's only a teenager. A crazy mixed-up orphan. Hardly a reliable prospect!"

Annabel shrugged.

"Then she ups and leaves me. I'll still have done the right thing for her."

Pauline was astonished by this reply. For a few moments she seemed lost for words.

"Annabel, you really are one impressive lady… I'm just beginning to realise…"

Annabel smiled at her, almost sympathetically.

"That's the nature of love, Pauline. There are no strings attached."

Taken aback, Pauline looked away, raised her arm and beckoned to the waiter. This gave her time to think before continuing. Her equanimity had been disturbed.

Annabel sat still in her armchair. She realised how much strain this callous negotiation was causing her. But she knew there was no other way to obtain Dolly's freedom. As her father used to tell her, sometimes you have to do bad things to achieve good things. Now she understood what he meant.

The waiter came over and spoke to Pauline, with whom he was obviously very familiar. She ordered two more glasses of wine and he went away. She looked hard at Annabel.

"It's getting a bit hot in here, don't you think? Let's go out to the pool."

"The pool?"

"Yes, there's a swimming pool up on the roof terrace, would you believe! A bit decadent, but very pleasant on hot days like this. I've used it a couple of times myself, though I'm not much of a swimmer."

"What a good idea. You lead the way."

They took their bags and walked up another flight of steps, which took them to a large roof terrace, protected by brick walls and black iron railings that offered a panoramic view of the rooftops and penthouses of Soho. The dazzling sunshine reflected back on the shimmering water of the pool, which was small and rectangular. The depth of the water was uniformly six feet. Along both lengths of the pool, surprisingly close to the edge, was an unbroken line of plastic chairs placed side by side to give spectators an intimate view of any swimmers who ventured in. It was perfectly designed for both voyeurs and exhibitionists. More than a dozen people had taken seats and were casually chatting and drinking. Annabel was unsurprised to see that Bernie and Sebastian were among the crowd, talking to a voluptuous young blonde in a white mini-dress who sat between them. Bernie looked over, grinned, and waved briefly.

At present the pool was empty and calm. Pauline and Annabel took a couple of chairs in an unoccupied area, diagonally opposite the part of the poolside where Bernie and his friends were sitting, in order to talk without being overheard. Annabel put on her sunglasses. Pauline seemed more serious and thoughtful than she had been in the lounge.

"Tell me, how are things with your boyfriend? Does he know what you've been getting up to with Dolly over the last few weeks?"

"Philip? I decided to bring our relationship to an end once I realised what my feelings for Dolly were. I don't care what he knows about the two of us."

"So you have no summer holiday planned?"

"No. The break I'd planned with Philip is obviously cancelled. He's not happy, but…"

"Maybe you can go on holiday with Dolly?"

Annabel smiled ironically.

"I'd love to take her abroad somewhere. But that doesn't depend on me, does it?"

The waiter arrived with the fresh glasses of wine. As they began sipping at their drinks, a young man and woman emerged from a glazed double-door, dressed in skimpy swimwear, and promptly dived into the pool together from the nearest end. In the enclosed space of the roof terrace the splashes made a big noise, and drew cheers and wolf-whistles from several of the spectators, who watched the swimmers thrusting along in the water with intense interest and amusement. The woman was topless and wore only a slender bikini bottom.

Pauline turned to Annabel.

"As I recall, you were an excellent swimmer at school. Do you still swim?"

"Yes, whenever I can."

"I'd love to watch you dive in and show everyone here just how good you are."

"But I haven't got any swimwear."

"Doesn't matter. Just take off your dress and swim in your underwear. Lots of people here do that. When the evening comes, most swimmers go in completely starkers. There's a room just over there where you can dry off. The waiter will give you a towel."

Annabel took off her sunglasses and smiled.

"Pauline, I seem to recall that I've done something very similar for you already. About twenty years ago…"

"Here at least you won't be diving off a bridge and risking your life!"

"True. But I'm not prepared to make an exhibition of myself to entertain a crowd of people. The answer is no." She put her sunglasses back on.

Pauline smiled. She seemed reassured by Annabel's refusal.

"Still a proper lady, I see."

"Still a proper lady."

"All right, Annabel. Let me put a more serious proposition to you."

"I'm listening."

"I was impressed by your remark downstairs about paying for Dolly's freedom regardless of whether she stays with you. It's made me realise that this whole thing is too important to be settled by money. I don't want you to pay me anything for Dolly."

Annabel stared at her. This was unexpected. As indeed was the next movement that Pauline made, which was to put her hand on the inside of Annabel's thigh, half-way between her knee and her crutch. The coldness of Pauline's hand startled Annabel, but she made no reaction. Pauline watched the swimmers in the pool as she spoke.

"Instead of money, I want you to agree to spend one night with me, alone. Just the two of us, at my studio-flat in Whitechapel. And to agree to do whatever I want while you're with me. If you do that, I'll release Dolly from all obligations and cancel her debt to me. The two of you will be free to live happily ever after. What do you think?"

Annabel's heart raced. She took off her sunglasses and stared at Pauline.

"Just like that?"

"Yes, just like that. But there are certain conditions."

"Such as?"

"Neither of us will tell Dolly about this… arrangement."

"All right. What else?"

"You will turn up for me dressed in your old St Margaret's School uniform. Do you still have it? I'd have thought you'd keep it, knowing your affection for the old school."

"I still have the blazer, blouse and skirt. They might still fit me, but they'd be very tight."

"The blazer, blouse and skirt are the most important things. The other items – the shoes, the white socks, the tights, the half-slip, the bra and knickers – you can get separately. But they'll have to be as close as possible to the original items – the things you wore when we had our little adventure on the bridge. As it's now summer, you can leave out the woolly jersey."

Pauline's icy cold hand moved further up Annabel's thigh, disappearing under the hem of the orange dress. Annabel felt Pauline's little finger brushing against her briefs, chilling her crutch, even though her legs remained tightly closed. She didn't move, aware of the importance and the delicacy of the moment. She was disorientated by this new approach from Pauline, which had completely wrong-footed her. She sipped awkwardly at her wine.

"What else?"

"I want you to wear a gold crucifix, just as you did back at St Margaret's. As I recall, you lost the one you were wearing at the time."

"Yes. I lost it in the river."

"Do you have another one?"

Annabel thought for a moment.

"I rarely wear a crucifix these days. But I have a very old one that my grandmother left to me."

"Excellent. That will do fine."

Annabel played for time. She felt the worry-worm twisting inside her, in response to Pauline's touch.

"Can I ask why you're imposing these conditions?"

"Let's say it's nostalgia for the old school. Nostalgia for the girls we used to be."

The cold edge of Pauline's finger now pressed hard against Annabel's pubis, through her silky briefs. Annabel caught her breath.

"I suppose you won't tell me what you have in mind?"

"No, not in detail. But you know what I want to do, Annabel. I want to fuck you. This time I'm going to take you properly. No need for anything crazy like jumping off a bridge."

Pauline's hand now pushed so hard against Annabel's crutch that she felt herself being forced back into her chair.

"Are you going to cane me, like Dolly?"

Pauline laughed and suddenly withdrew her hand. She drank briefly from her wine glass.

"Why not? Would you be prepared to take a good caning to win Dolly?"

"Yes. I'd take it if I had to."

"And a good fucking?"

"And a good fucking. If I agree to your terms."

"All right, darling. Take your time and think about it. Send me a letter within a week, with a one-word reply. Yes or No. You decide."

"That's it? No other terms or conditions?"

Pauline shook her head. She reached into her bag and handed Annabel the envelope with the money.

"Here. This proves how serious I am. If you want to take Dolly from me, it's you or nothing. That's the deal. You can take it or leave it. And you can take or leave Dolly. It's up to you. In the meantime, you can have the little slut for as long as you want this weekend, in exchange for complying with the request I made earlier – a demonstration of your swimming prowess. Right here and now. In front of everybody. As soon as the pool is free."

Annabel didn't know what to do or say. Clearly the money was now irrelevant. After a couple of moments she took the envelope and put it back into her handbag.

Pauline leaned back and stretched out her legs. In less than a minute the two swimmers had finished and hauled themselves from the pool immediately in front of Pauline and Annabel, who were splashed with a little of the water that they brought out with them. The woman's nipples were stiff and erect and she was giggling uncontrollably. There was a raucous round of applause from the spectators and more whistles as the couple ran back hand-in-hand to the changing-room.

Pauline laughed and flicked the water from her legs. She looked pointedly at Annabel.

"Your turn, darling." She gestured towards the swimming pool.

Annabel had little choice. She knew she had to be with Dolly at the weekend. After a short pause, she took off her watch, her engagement ring, and the circle of beads around her neck. She took off her ear-rings. She leaned down to unstrap and kick off her high-heeled sandals. Then she stood up and turned her back on Pauline, who gazed at her enthralled as she proceeded to unzip the short orange dress from behind and let it drop to her feet. Now she was naked apart from her silky yellow briefs. There was a sudden murmur and a few gasps from around the pool as Annabel made her way gingerly to the nearest end, uncomfortably aware of her jiggling breasts and the hard slippery tiles under her bare feet. As she turned to face the length of the pool, there was an outburst of applause and wolf-whistling, much louder than before. She saw Pauline staring at her with undisguised elation, long bony hands folded as if in prayer. She tried to blank the presence of Bernie and his friends from her mind as she stepped forward to the poolside edge.

Annabel looked up at the sunny sky, then down at the clean blue water. She pulled the flimsy briefs higher up her hips, and up between her buttocks, to prevent them coming off in the water. This exposed a fuzz of dark pubic hair at both sides of the yellow fabric. There was a hubbub of approval and yet more shrill whistling from the spectators. All of them were watching her, waiting for her... all of them poised so indecently close to the pool. To her surprise, she felt a thrill of excitement surging in her belly. The worry-worm had disappeared. The time had come to take the plunge. To be a reckless girl again. She took a deep breath, closed her eyes, opened her arms and flung herself headlong into the water.

The following Saturday Annabel took Dolly to Oxford and showed her around the city centre. This was one of the many places that the girl had never visited before and she enjoyed herself enormously, although her revealing black PVC mini-dress (worn to please Annabel) was hardly in keeping with the cultural tone of the ancient colleges. For her part, Dolly couldn't help noting that her lover was subdued and lost in thought throughout the day, even though Annabel treated her kindly and bought her several gifts and a fine restaurant meal. Late in the evening they were back in the flat at Earls Court, lying naked side by side on the bed. For a while, at Dolly's insistence, they looked through some of Annabel's many autobiographical photo-albums. In due course Annabel closed the albums and took her partner by the hand.

"Dolly, forgive me for asking – but what kind of evidence does Pauline hold against you?"

Dolly gently ran her finger around Annabel's palm. She took her time to reply.

"She can get Bernie and his friends to stitch me up, anytime. Bernie is friendly with a lot of policemen, who he can influence because he's done favours for them. You wouldn't believe how corrupt they are. They could set me up any which way they wanted. They know a lot of drug dealers. Bernie actually controls a lot of the dealers himself. They could slaughter me."

"I see. You can't influence Bernie yourself in any way?"

Dolly laughed.

"No. I'm just a young tart he likes to fuck. His girlfriend, Francine, joins in a lot of the time. She was a prostitute when she was younger. She likes weak helpless girls. Sometimes…"

"Go on, tell me."

"Sometimes other people in his gang spend the night with me, after giving me drugs. Some nights I'll be done by two guys at a time… or a guy and his girlfriend."

"You poor thing. What about your… health?"

"The guys do use condoms – well, mostly – and Paulie gets me checked out all the time at an STD clinic. She's concerned about her own health as well."

"I should hope so. What else do you have to do for her?"

"I'm more worried about what she wants me to do in the next

couple of months. Bernie's started talking to people in Soho and Eastern Europe about putting me in porn films. Proper hard-core stuff, where I get whipped and fucked by a whole gang of men."

"Oh Dolly, that's just awful! We mustn't allow that to happen. It would completely ruin your future!"

"I know. But what can I do?"

Annabel squeezed her hand. She was increasingly alarmed by what she was hearing.

"Would Pauline really put you in prison if you ran away from her?"

Dolly nodded glumly.

"Yes, she would. She told me she'd track me down and get me put away for five years. She's not bullshitting either. I know how ruthless she can be. I'm scared of going to prison… having all my freedom taken away. I know I'd be bullied non-stop, like I've been everywhere else. You're about the only person I've met who treats me like I really count for anything."

Annabel leaned over and kissed her.

"My poor darling. *I'd* hate to be in prison as well."

"I just want to be with you. I feel safe here with you. It's like having a real home at last."

"Dolly, what would you do if you lived here with me? All the time? Wouldn't you feel like a prisoner as well, only in a nicer place?"

Dolly shook her head. Suddenly she grinned, mischievously.

"Shall I tell you my fantasy?"

"Oh, please do…"

"All right. Lie on your back."

Annabel obeyed. Now animated, Dolly climbed on top of her and pinned down her wrists on the pillow, at either side of her head. Triumphantly she sat astride her belly.

"In my fantasy – I'd make you *my* prisoner and I'd be your guard.

You'd be Annabel James, Prisoner Number five-four-three-two-one."

"Oh no! Would I have any chance of escaping?"

"No, no chance at all! You'd be my prisoner for life…"

"For life? Oh Lord, that's a long sentence. What would my jailer do with me for all that time?"

"I'd keep you all naked on a golden chain, with a golden collar round your neck, and I'd guard you day and night, so I'd know you were always close to me, and I could always touch you when I wanted to. I'd feed you, and wash you, and brush your hair, and take you to the bathroom and… and I'd watch you pee while you squat in the shower, and then I'd wipe your pussy for you afterwards. And then I'd kiss you all over and tell you how beautiful you are. Would you like that?"

"Oh yes. I think I'd love being your prisoner. But then who's going to do anything for you?"

Dolly released Annabel's wrists and slowly began squeezing her breasts, as if trying to draw something from them. Her voice dropped.

"Would you… would *you* do all those things for *me*?"

"Yes, gladly."

"Would you really? For a little brat like me?"

"Yes… especially for a little brat like you." She looked unwaveringly at Dolly and gently stroked her lissom hips. In the semi-darkness she could see Dolly's eyes glistening.

"Annabel… I've gone all hot and wet."

Annabel felt Dolly's wetness on her navel and swiftly grew aroused herself. She opened her thighs and her hands closed around the girl's buttocks as she drew her down.

"Come to me, Dolly… come closer."

Dolly leaned down between her lover's legs until her face almost touched Annabel's. In the dim light, Annabel thought she was looking at a mirror image of herself… herself as a girl.

"I want to be your prisoner for life," whispered Dolly, gazing into the tawny eyes. "I want to be with you forever… always and forever."

"Then come into me, my baby," breathed Annabel. "I want you inside me forever."

They kissed ecstatically, their tongues hungrily jabbing and flicking as their mouths opened wide and pressed together. Annabel drew her knees up and groaned with joy as Dolly's dainty fingers slid smoothly into her vagina. Dolly was always amazed by how quickly her lover was ready for her. Annabel's warm welcoming body was the only real home she had ever known. And her face at the moment of orgasm was the only glimpse of Heaven that Dolly would ever want.

A few hours later, in the middle of the night, Annabel woke. Her mind was still troubled. Dolly lay slumbering serenely against her ribs. She got out of bed and went to the bathroom to relieve herself on the toilet. Then she went to the kitchen and poured herself a glass of wine. She took this into the lounge and stood by the window, gazing down at the flashing lights of the endless London traffic. The lights reflected her own turmoil.

She contemplated the irony of being in virtually the same position as twenty years ago, when Pauline had blackmailed her after overhearing her with Mr Murray. But there was a big difference. Last time she had succumbed to Pauline in a desperate bid to save herself from ruin. This time she was going to take the initiative and offer herself in order to save someone else. It was a much worthier motive. She remembered as a young child having fantasies of offering herself as a sacrifice in exchange for the life of a dashing hero, who would mourn her forever afterwards. These became guilty sexual fantasies when she was eleven and twelve, and fortunately faded as she grew older and stepped into the role of being a hero herself, someone to be admired and imitated by others. She wondered now whether her self-destructive urges had ever really gone away. Perhaps they had just gone into hiding to wait for the right circumstances to re-activate them. Then she realised that this was different: she was now the sacrifice *and* the hero, offering herself for someone who was weak and defenceless. This was what she had always wanted to do: be strong and noble for someone else, then be martyred to show her eternal devotion. She realised that the masculine and feminine sides of her personality had now come together as one. This conjunction of the two halves was what Miriam had overlooked in their conversation a few weeks earlier. Now Annabel understood why one of her greatest inspirations had always been Joan of Arc, to whom Sister Helena had introduced her many years ago at St Margaret's. Joan had likewise fused together her masculine and feminine halves, and in doing so had discovered her Divine Self. Annabel was suddenly elated by the realisation that she had discovered hers.

She heard Dolly stirring and turning over in the bed, and realised that the truth was actually much simpler. She was going to sacrifice herself for someone she loved – more than anyone she had loved before, except possibly her father. Someone she had vowed to save, whatever it took. All her life Annabel had been the recipient of the desires of others, saying yes or no as the fancy took her, but always passive. This time *she* was playing the active part, to win someone that *she* desired. She was making the running, taking the risks. Maybe that was the hallmark of genuine love.

Did she have any choice but to accept Pauline's proposal? To pay her price? She knew that this time she would be subjected to many hours of painful and degrading abuse. However much it hurt her pride, and however much it tormented her body, she would have to submit to being Pauline's victim once again. But now, after twenty years of accumulated sexual experience, she would be able to withstand whatever her adversary did to her. She had survived the last ordeal and would survive this one. She gazed at Pauline's hockey stick, standing upright by the curtain a couple of feet from her. It hadn't been a peace offering after all – it had in fact turned out to be a declaration of war. A war that she had no chance of winning, as her capitulation at the swimming pool had demonstrated. But her defeat would at least bring about Dolly's liberation.

She sipped at the wine and moved over to a cabinet in the corner of the room. She pulled open a small drawer and took out a jewellery box. Inside were a number of family heirlooms, mainly trinkets of sentimental value. The largest item was the heavy ornate gold crucifix that Grandma Giuliana had left her when she was a child. She hadn't looked at it for years. Now she lifted it up and inspected the finely carved figure of the Saviour on the Cross, showing the patient artistry of a more devout and reverential era. The whole item was almost four inches long, as large as the crosses that the Sisters at St Margaret's used to wear. No doubt it was another sacrifice that she would have to make. She hoped Grandma would forgive her.

"Can't you sleep, Annabel?"

Dolly had woken up and come into the lounge. She was rubbing her eyes.

"No. I've got a lot on my mind."

"I know. You've been worried about something all day. What is it?"

Annabel put the crucifix back in the jewellery box and closed the lid.

"I can't tell you now. But I will when it's all over."

Dolly walked across the lounge and put her arms around Annabel's waist. Her head nuzzled against her shoulder.

"I don't like sleeping without you. Come back to bed and hold me."

Annabel wrapped her arms around the girl, tighter than ever before. Dolly moaned contentedly. They had become the yolk and the white of the same egg. Annabel prayed that it wouldn't be broken.

A couple of days later, on Tuesday morning, Pauline was in her studio, dressed in her denim overalls, working out the best colour scheme for her latest acrylic painting, a large picture of a nude adolescent girl riding a gigantic hockey stick as if it were a rocking horse. As usual, Dolly brought the day's post into the studio and left it on the table.

"It's looking good, Paulie," she said approvingly, nodding at the painting.

"Thank you, Sweetheart," said Pauline. "You see, you've inspired me yet again."

As Dolly went up close to the painting to admire her own image, Pauline picked up the half dozen items of post on the table. One small envelope marked Special Delivery immediately caught her eye and she opened it. There was a single sheet of folded pink notepaper, which she opened out. On it was handwritten in black ink:

*Yes*

*Annabel*

Pauline took a deep breath and smiled triumphantly.

"What is it, Paulie?" asked Dolly, looking round at her. "Some good news?"

"Oh yes," replied Pauline. "Wonderful news!"

# XI

## FULL PAYMENT

CLAD IN HER St Margaret's uniform, Annabel left the School behind her and hurried through the woods as the evening light faded. She was determined not to lose the girl, who was moving ahead fast, trying to escape. She had stolen Annabel's hockey stick. Annabel found the path and quickened her step, now beginning to run. The path straightened and she started to gain ground on the girl, who was much smaller and younger than her. Then the view opened out onto the gorge and Annabel saw that it was the path over the old bridge, which looked hoary and crumbling and sinister in the evening light. The girl was standing at the other end of the bridge, just where the path entered the woods again at the other side of the gorge. She turned to face Annabel. It was Dolly, smiling sweetly. She was dressed in a white blouse and a tiny tartan skirt. She lifted her skirt and began to rub the oversized hockey stick against her shaven crutch, moaning with indecent pleasure as it slid back and forth over her smooth vagina. She seemed to be riding it with great expertise. As the girl stared at Annabel, still smiling, a billowing dark cloud emerged from the jungle of weeds on the granite embankment a short way downriver, and rose with frightful speed all the way up to the level of the treetops that overlooked the bridge. Abruptly the sky darkened. Nonetheless Annabel advanced towards the girl, determined to retrieve her hockey stick. As she reached the middle of the bridge, a brilliant fork of lightning shot out from the black cloud and struck the path a couple of feet in front of her, burning into the stone paving like a laser beam. The bridge quaked horribly with a loud rumbling noise like thunder and started to crumble and break just in front of her feet, which she suddenly noticed were bare. To her horror, she realised she was now entirely naked. Then the ground beneath her fell apart completely, and she saw in the river rushing far below her a monstrous octopus, its huge mouth wide open, slavering and hissing as it waited for her to fall. As she looked once more at Dolly, who had now raised the hockey stick above her head like a trophy and was laughing, Annabel felt herself plunge down, helplessly, in slow motion. The tentacles of the monster waved wildly and reached up to embrace her as she descended into the gigantic mouth. Her legs disappeared into the slimy orifice; then she was sucked into it up to her waist. She could feel the jaws of the octopus squeezing tighter and tighter all over her body, drawing her down to her doom. She struggled valiantly and thrashed her arms, but stood no chance against the powerful beast. It drew her down further and further until only her head remained above the mouth. Finally she screamed as the jaws closed above her and everything went dark. Her last action was a desperate thrashing kick into the blackness, which succeeded in waking her up. She gasped and rolled over into the duvet, her heart pounding. She kicked the duvet again, to reassure herself that she had escaped. She vowed never to return to the bridge again.

It was the middle of the night. The night before the day on which she would pay Pauline's price.

Philip arrived home at six in the evening. He opened the door to his flat and saw the usual pile of daily post on the floor. He picked up the items and immediately recognised Annabel's bold handwriting on the smallest of the envelopes. He threw down his briefcase and hurried over to an armchair in the lounge.

He tore open the envelope and unfolded the pink notepaper.

*My darling Phil*

*Please forgive me for my show of anger in the restaurant. I appreciate why you were so concerned about me and I know what you really feel for me. I'm so sorry it didn't work out for us. One day I hope you'll understand the reasons for what I've done.*

> *Thank you for everything.*
> *All my love –*
> *Annabel*

Wearily Philip dropped the letter to the floor. Now he knew for sure it was all over: her gracious valediction was far more conclusive than her angry exit from the restaurant. He put his head in his hands and sighed heavily. He wondered whether she herself understood the reasons for what she was doing.

Annabel looked at her watch as the taxi-cab turned from Commercial Road into the side street. It was eight o'clock; an hour after sunset at the end of August. The old nineteenth-century warehouses, now converted to residential use, towered above the taxi on both sides. The narrow crooked street was already draped in shadows, inadequately dispelled by the drab street lights. Cars were parked on both sides of the road, slowing the driver's approach to the railway bridge that hung low over the street. Finally they arrived at the address. The driver turned round to Annabel, who was in the back of the cab.

"Here we are, madam."

Annabel leaned forward and gave him a banknote.

"Keep the change."

"Many thanks. Is it a fancy dress party, then?"

"Pardon?"

The driver nodded at the school uniform. He stared approvingly at the navy blue blazer, with its proud St Margaret's badge, the sky blue blouse, the grey skirt and the knee-high white socks. He was amused and titillated to see a woman of Annabel's age dressed in such a manner.

"Oh yes, of course," smiled Annabel. "It's a fancy dress party."

"Mmm… wouldn't mind going there myself. Pity I've got more jobs waiting. Have a good time, love."

"Thanks."

Annabel clambered awkwardly out of the cab, which promptly drove off.

The old St Margaret's uniform was as uncomfortable as she had feared it would be. She hadn't put on much weight since her school days, and had had no children to enlarge her body, but it was nonetheless a very tight fit. Her shoulders and arms felt stiff and constricted in the polyester blazer. The buttons on the sky-blue blouse were almost popping, and showing bits of her white bra and her skin as the placket line between each button was pulled apart by the pressure of her chest. Her breasts had clearly grown larger with age. As had her midriff: the skirt felt like a corset around her mature hips, and the zip at the back felt close to bursting. She was uncomfortably aware of the clingy nylon tights and the cotton socks encasing her calves all the way up to the knees. Even the flat black shoes felt too small. The weather was still hot and she was again perspiring. But some of this was undoubtedly caused by the anxiety she felt about the next twelve hours. Here she was, once again… at Pauline's mercy. The worry-worm was working overtime. Her mouth felt dry. There was no turning back now.

An invisible train rumbled over the nearby bridge, adding to the menacing atmosphere. The ageing plaster that covered the frontage of the premises was cracked and broken, crumbling away like infected skin, revealing the gnarled brickwork of a long-dead era. Pauline could hardly have chosen a more forbidding place to live and work. In fact, that was probably why she *had* chosen it. Annabel now took one last item from the pocket of her blazer: the gold crucifix from Grandma. She secured the chain around her neck and placed the cross on her chest, where it dangled uneasily over the exposed patch of white brassiere. She had left Dolly's engagement ring at home. Tonight she knew she would have to break the promise that she had made to her lover.

The entrance was a large heavy black door with a couple of steps leading up straight from the street. The ground floor windows were boarded up. Annabel took a few deep breaths to compose herself. She had eaten nothing since the morning, so as to reduce the pressure on her digestive system for what was going to be a testing night. She didn't want to risk any accident that would heap further indignity upon her. But she was determined to pass the test that lay ahead, whatever it was, and to win the prize that awaited her. The greater the ordeal, the greater her achievement. With this positive thought in her mind, Annabel pressed the button marked "P. Barrie".

After a few moments came the reply.

*"Annabel?"*

"Yes."

*"Come on up, my dear. Take the stairs to the first floor…"*

The entrance door clicked open and she pushed her way in. A shadowy stone stairwell led off to the right and she soon climbed to the first floor lobby. Pauline was waiting for her in the doorway of her flat, dressed in a long full-sleeved dark green gown, leaning against the door jamb and looking relaxed as she smoked a cigarette. She smiled broadly as Annabel arrived, clearly savouring the moment.

"Lovely to see you, Annabel. Oh my God – you look absolutely *divine* dressed like that, just as you did at St Margaret's. Come on in and let me admire you."

After pausing in a small reception hall, where Pauline spent some time gasping with pleasure at the sight of Annabel's uniform, they walked into the lounge, a very large square room with a high ceiling and tall narrow windows. The curtains were drawn but the room was brightly illuminated by neon lights set in round metal lamps that hung from chains in the ceiling. Annabel was astonished by what she saw on the whitewashed brick walls: they were covered with dozens of silkscreens of Dolly's caned buttocks, in a variety of sizes, patterns and colours. At a rough guess, Annabel estimated there were about fifty of them. She looked quizzically at Pauline, who grinned back at her.

"I put the silkscreens up to make you feel at home, darling. The sight of Dolly's cute little arse should remind you of what you've come here for."

"Very thoughtful. But I've already seen your handiwork – in the flesh."

"So I understand. My goodness, Annabel, you look eminently cane-worthy yourself in that uniform."

"I assume that's why I'm wearing it."

Pauline chuckled, somewhat loudly. Annabel could see that her eyes looked large and glazed, just as they had during their conversation at the Gallery some weeks ago. Then Pauline noticed the large crucifix on Annabel's chest. She touched the figure of Christ with one finger.

"What a beautiful piece of jewellery! I love antiques. Thank you so much for bringing it."

"I'm glad you approve." Annabel swallowed hard. Her mouth was now very dry.

"You look a tad thirsty. Can I get you a glass of wine?" asked Pauline solicitously. "There's an excellent Rioja I opened just an hour ago. Let's both give it a try."

"Yes, thanks – I'd love a glass."

As Pauline went over to a cabinet to pour the wine, Annabel stood by the gnarled oak coffee table, not sure what to do or where to go, feeling foolish in her ill-fitting uniform. She took in the rest of the lounge: a large high bookcase, heavy old-fashioned sofa and armchairs, tall wooden standing lamps, ornate side tables with exotic pot plants. Clearly Pauline had a pronounced if inconsistent taste for antique furniture. The place smelled of decaying leather, mingled with a faint odour of sickly-sweet incense. The massive stuffed head of a black goat glared down at her from the wall facing the well-worn sofa. At the far end of the lounge a spiral staircase, obviously a recent construction, wound its way up to the floor above. Annabel wondered whether she was destined to climb those stairs later in the evening. What torment might be waiting for her up there? She took a deep breath.

Pauline gave her the wine, which filled half the glass, and gestured towards an armchair. Annabel sat down, knees together, grateful for at least a civilised start to the proceedings. She sipped at the wine. It was a fine strong Rioja. Pauline sat on the sofa. Her bare feet rested on the polished floorboards.

"Did you comply with all my requirements?"

"Yes," replied Annabel. "I've said nothing to Dolly or anyone else."

"Good. Isn't it more fun to abandon yourself to the experience completely? It's the thrill of performing without a safety net."

"Maybe so. I can't say it's exactly a thrill being here in these circum-stances. But I'm ready to play your game – whatever it may be."

"Good girl!" Pauline gazed at her like a predatory bird sizing up its prey.

Annabel took a longer sip of the wine. It certainly was strong stuff – she felt her head reacting to it already. This was of course the result of drinking on an empty stomach. At least it had the effect of calming her quickly.

"By the way, Dolly is spending the night with Bernie," went on Pauline. "I thought that might be the best thing for everyone, given our rendezvous here tonight."

Annabel was far from happy to hear this news. She took another sip of the wine.

"I trust this will be the last time she sees Bernie? If our agreement is to be binding?"

"Oh yes, it will be the last time," replied Pauline. "But Bernie doesn't know that."

Annabel's unease grew.

"Where are they?"

"At his flat in Soho. With Sebastian and Bernie's girlfriend, Francine – she really enjoys the company of masochistic young girls. Should be quite a party."

"Pauline," smiled Annabel grimly, "I get the impression you're doing your best to upset me."

"Not at all. I'm just trying to get you into the right mood. We have our own little party to enjoy tonight."

Annabel drank the remainder of the wine, emptying the glass. She decided it was best to confront her fate without fear or hesitation, as Sister Helena had advised.

"All right. I'm ready to start partying whenever you are."

Pauline smiled warmly.

"I knew you would be. Put the glass down, Annabel, and come over here. I want you to stand right in front of me."

As she rose to her feet, Annabel felt a sudden giddiness come over her. She swayed for a moment and touched the side of her head.

"That wine is pretty strong," said Pauline. "Especially if you haven't eaten for a while."

"I'll be all right," replied Annabel. She walked over to the sofa to stand directly in front of Pauline. Her arms hung loosely by her side as she looked down at her old adversary. Pauline's big eyes were shining. Appreciatively she inspected Annabel's uniform. The hem of the skirt was a few inches above the knee.

"Take off that heavy old blazer, my dear. You must be sweating to death in it."

Annabel was happy to comply. She dropped the blazer to the floor.

"How wonderful to see you again in these clothes. Genuine St Margaret's stock. What memories they bring back..." She lifted the grey skirt to sniff it, exposing the white petticoat beneath. Her other arm reached around Annabel's bottom and touched the zip.

"My God, your skirt is so *tight*!" Annabel felt the hand press into her backside and squeeze.

"And that blouse as well," continued Pauline. "It looks fit to burst under the pressure of those big boobies!"

Pauline moved her hand up to flick open the top three buttons of the sky-blue blouse, under the crucifix, revealing the white bra. Then she squeezed one of the curvaceous breasts. Annabel looked at her impassively. She felt oddly tired and drained of energy. But for this reason, the fondling didn't cause her any agitation. Pauline withdrew her hands for a moment.

"Open your legs wider, darling."

Annabel did as instructed. The flat shoes stood almost a metre apart and the skirt and petticoat rose higher.

"Now we're going to have a little quiz. Or should I say an interrogation... all about your life, your past, your sweet lovely self. I'll ask the questions and you'll give me the answers. No talking back. Just the true and correct answers. Understood?"

"Yes."

Pauline's hand now eased up under Annabel's skirt and petticoat until it reached the hot crutch of her tights. The hand moved up higher and harder until it was pressing on the gusset of Annabel's knickers. She breathed deeply and closed her eyes; she swayed slightly.

"First question, then. What's your full name?"

Annabel opened her eyes and looked at Pauline. She seemed oddly out of focus.

"Annabel Maria James."

Pauline's other hand went up behind the outside of the skirt and started tugging at the stiff zip. After a couple of pulls it gave and came down. Annabel felt the skirt loosen around her hips – something of a relief.

"What's your father's name? What did he do for a living?"

"Frank Reginald James. He was a Commander in the Royal Navy."

Pauline now eased down the skirt until it reached Annabel's ankles. She stroked the silky half-slip petticoat. The hem was decorated with fine lace.

"Is he still alive?"

"No. He died in a car crash when I was nineteen."

"Oh, how sad. Were you close to him?"

"Yes, very close. I was traumatised by his death – it was so sudden and shocking. I thought he was indestructible. He was my hero. He was the biggest influence on my life."

"Yes – I can see he must have been. And I'm sure you were always Daddy's Princess."

"Yes… always."

Pauline eased the slip down until it joined the grey skirt on the floor. Annabel stood in her tan-coloured tights, displaying a pair of small white cotton knickers under the sheer nylon hose. To her surprise, she felt entirely relaxed about showing her body to Pauline.

"Now tell me about your mother."

"Her name is Clara. She's from the Italian side of the family – from Grandma Giuliana, who I was also very close to…"

Pauline undid the remaining buttons of the blouse save the bottom one, which held the lower part of the shirt tightly in place as she pulled the rest of it down over the back of Annabel's shoulders. This had the effect of pinning her arms slightly behind her back. The bra lifted the bosom up and forward, especially when Annabel breathed in deeply. The crucifix nestled in her cleavage.

"What did your mother do?" asked Pauline, putting both hands over the bra and squeezing.

Annabel moaned. The pressure on her breasts was delightful, even though the hands were cold.

"She was an air stewardess. She gave up the job to raise me and my brother. After my father died, she became an alcoholic. I've always done the best I can for her…"

"I'm sure you have, Annabel. But now I want to get more intimate. I want you to tell me about your sex life."

"All right."

"How many sexual partners have you had?"

"I think… about forty in all."

Pauline laughed and sat back on the sofa.

"Annabel! Forty! I can't believe you've been such a bad girl! Our Virgin Saint Margaret would *not* approve!"

Annabel felt embarrassed, as if she had truly been a naughty girl. She tried to justify herself.

"Most of them were short term. Many of them at university and

185

Medical School. And when I worked at various hospitals. Medics are much hornier than people realise…"

"Obviously they are. And not just the nurses, it appears! How many serious or long-term relationships have you had?"

"Half a dozen. I was married once, for six years. I was faithful to my husband… even though the marriage was unhappy most of the time."

Pauline leaned forward again. She put her fingers under the waistline top of the tights and began to slide them down over the knickers, which slipped down slightly as a result. The upper part of Annabel's buttocks and her dark pubic hair peeped out above the knicker-elastic. Pauline leaned further forward to sniff the white cotton over her genitals. Annabel felt herself growing weak and strangely calm. She was happy to go along with whatever Pauline wanted to do. It was actually pleasurable to give in and play the game…

Pauline pulled and rolled the nylon hose down to Annabel's knees and left the tights there, held in place by her widely parted legs.

"Have you ever had a lesbian lover? Apart from Dolly?"

"Yes. One. She was my tutor at Oxford."

Pauline started rubbing the firm sun-tanned thighs, now naked in front of her.

"Interesting. Tell me more about her – and what you did together."

"Her name was Miriam. She seduced me and we had a secret affair for eight months. I was dominated by her… by her intellect and her energy. In the end I had to break away from her to preserve my individuality… to assert myself."

"Did you ever tell anyone about her?"

"No. Never."

"Did you have a boyfriend at the same time?"

"Yes. I had three or four. But I never told any of them about Miriam."

Pauline reached up and put her hands behind Annabel's ribs and her pinioned arms. Carefully she unhooked the bra. It slipped down and Pauline lifted the lacy cups to expose the breasts, which sagged slightly downwards. Pauline bypassed the crucifix and ran her finger over one of the large nipples, which were hard and erect. Annabel moaned and looked straight at her.

"Pauline, what's happening? I feel strange…it isn't just the wine."

"Don't worry. I put a little… relaxant at the bottom of your wineglass. Just to get you into the party mood. It won't harm you, darling."

"You've drugged me, you bitch…"

"Hush, Annabel! Just go with it. I want you to enjoy what we're doing tonight, instead of fighting against it. You are enjoying it, aren't you?"

"Yes, but… it's not right."

"If it feels good, it must be right. Trust me, darling. Just concentrate on answering my questions. I want to find out all about you. I've always wanted to know your secrets, Annabel. Now I'm going to find out. This is part of the deal – so play the game. All right?"

"All right…"

Pauline now put the fingers of both hands under the elastic top of Annabel's knickers and slowly, gently eased down the soft white cotton. The pubic hair and then the lips of the vulva were exposed as she slipped the briefs down to the knees, to rest on the nylon hose already there. The elastic was stretched as far as it would go without tearing. Pauline moaned with satisfaction when she saw the heavy streak of moist amber on the inside of the white gusset. She could smell the animal scent of Annabel's arousal. She ran her finger over the thick pubic hair.

In a dreamy, almost detached state, Annabel looked down at her knickers, now pulled all the way down to her knees, and at her heavy breasts swinging slowly from side to side, the gold crucifix dangling over them, and realised the full extent of her subjection and her humiliation. She was unable to move her arms, which were pinned around her back, and unable to send any energy to her legs. She felt like a helpless schoolgirl being abused by an adult. Intrigued, she watched as Pauline raised the middle finger of her hand to her pussy and then felt a sharp nervous shock run through her groin as it slid easily into her wet tender membranes. She arched her back and groaned as the whole of Pauline's finger now pushed up inside her.

"Now, Annabel, tell me what kind of sex you most enjoy."

"I enjoy…. aahh… I enjoy good sex under a strong man…. oooh! A hard cock pushing into me and drilling me non-stop until I come…"

Now the finger was twisting and wriggling inside her… Pauline knew exactly where to find her most sensitive spot. Annabel's nerves thrilled to the touch.

"Do you like oral sex? Being licked to a total frenzy?"

"Yes – I like it… I like it… aahh!"

"I knew you did…"

Pauline eased her three middle fingers into Annabel's pussy, which was now thoroughly wet. With her other hand she grabbed one of the breasts and squeezed it hard. Annabel winced and looked into Pauline's eyes.

"*You're* a whore too, Annabel. Aren't we all, when it comes down to it?"

Wearily Annabel shook her head.

"Don't lie, darling. I saw how turned on you were when you stripped at the swimming pool."

Annabel smiled weakly. She felt her mouth starting to sag.

"Not as turned on as you were!"

Now Pauline smiled.

"You're damn right! I almost came in my chair when you hoisted up those little silk panties and showed everyone your pussy hair. Only a tart would do that!" She twisted her hand upwards to apply pressure to Annabel's clitoris.

Annabel closed her eyes and sighed with pleasure. Her legs were getting weaker by the moment. As her knees started to bend, the rolled-down knickers and tights began to slip below them. The material was now held up only by the white socks that firmly gripped her calves. Pauline resumed her attack, squeezing Annabel's breast harder.

"Now tell me about Mr Murray. When he fucked you in the Biology Lab."

"Yes... aah!"

"How many times had he fucked you before I overheard you that afternoon?"

"A few times.... five or six times.... oooh!"

"You convent school slut! Getting fucked by a teacher! And everyone thinking you were so virtuous and perfect! You were barely sixteen, you whore!"

"You can call me what you want," moaned Annabel, growing ever more giddy and weak. "It won't make any difference...!"

In response to this, Pauline inserted all the fingers of her hand into Annabel and pushed up hard. Annabel groaned.

"Next question. Our sweet little Dolly. Do you truly love her?"

"You know I do. That's the reason I'm here."

"So it is – you fool!"

Pauline's free hand gripped tighter on Annabel's breast, her finger and thumb pinching and pulling her nipple until it was twisted completely out of shape.

"Ohh... oww!"

"So tell me how you fuck Dolly."

Annabel gasped, then forced a weak grin as she looked Pauline in the eye.

"I don't. She fucks me!"

Pauline grinned back.

"I know she fucks you. Don't you think she hasn't told me that? I just wanted to hear you say it, you lesbian slut."

Annabel shook her head.

"It doesn't matter about the fucking. All I want is Dolly…"

"Don't lie to me!" snapped Pauline. "You love being fucked!"

To prove her point, she rammed Annabel's vagina hard, vigorously sliding in and out with the whole of her long bony hand. Annabel cried out; her knees buckled and started to tremble. She was losing all stability as the jabbing hand and the insidious drug drained more and more of her strength. The worry-worm had disappeared, to be replaced by a warm numbness that was making her dissolve inside and float down to the floor. Yet she could feel every one of Pauline's invading fingers, squirming and thrusting like demons inside her belly, plucking mercilessly at her unguarded womb. She had no more strength to resist. As she surrendered to the brutal invasion, she felt a hot glowing furnace come to life somewhere in the darkest depth of her bowels… a fireball billowing outwards and upwards and filling her abdomen… Suddenly her back shot up straight and hard as the fireball erupted into an orgasm, and she felt herself disintegrating inside as the spasms surged all over her body. She looked up at the high white ceiling as her eyes crossed and her mouth gaped wide. She was now sinking as she climaxed, Pauline leaning forward and downwards from the sofa to accompany her as she twitched and jerked into one spasm after another. Finally she let out a long deep groan and her knees hit the wooden floorboards with a heavy thud. At the periphery of her vision she could see Pauline grinning, eyes staring wildly as she gloried in her triumph. One more spasm shot through her, and Annabel gasped one last time. She was completely spent.

Pauline's free hand now grabbed the hair on the top of her head while her other hand remained pushed up all the way into her vagina, so that Annabel stayed down on her knees, arms pinned helplessly under her blouse at either side. The floor felt cruelly hard. Still dazed and breathless and trembling from her orgasm, held up by her hair like a naughty child, Annabel looked wearily into the smirking face of her conqueror. She felt this was a defeat not just for her but also for St Margaret's, whose disgraced uniform hung in disarray from her exhausted body. She looked down at herself and saw the crucifix swaying from side to side over her bare breasts, the figure of the Saviour glinting in the neon light. She closed her eyes and silently begged forgiveness from Sister Helena. Finally she let go and surrendered to Pauline, falling forward into her arms as she passed out.

The four party revellers at Bernie's penthouse flat in Soho had long since shed all their clothes. A suitable bump-and-grind soundtrack throbbed across the spacious lounge from the large hi-fi speakers. A dozen or more *Lovelines* prints adorned the walls.

Nicely dosed up on Bernie's coke, Dolly had her eyes shut and was focusing her mind on the "Going Down" exhibit at the Black Sun Gallery while she sat upright on Sebastian and calmly rode back and forth on his sturdy penis. He lay on his back on the thick carpet with a wide grin on his face. His hands reached up to Dolly's chest and fondled her petite breasts. Her dark hair had been braided into two long thick pigtails that hung down over her chest.

Her reverie was rudely interrupted by a snappy lash across the back from Bernie's black leather riding crop.

"Aahh! Shit!"

Slightly annoyed, she opened her eyes and looked up at Bernie. The grin on his face was even bigger than Sebastian's.

"Time for another work-out, Little Dolly!"

"Fucking hell, Bernie! There's nowhere left to whack!" she protested.

Bernie scowled. He could see what she meant. During the last two hours he had decorated her lithe body with the full range of his black leather flogging instruments, and she was a mass of purple welts and patches from collar-bone to foot.

"I bet I can find somewhere I haven't whacked," he grinned again.

"If you really *must*," replied Dolly. With the amount of coke she'd taken this evening, she was actually enjoying the physical thrill of being beaten, but she didn't want Bernie to know that and have it too easy. If she made a fuss about the flogging, he'd keep her topped up with his high-grade white powder all through the night. She raised her arms in a gesture of surrender to take the next set of lashes and suddenly grew excited again.

As Bernie pondered where to aim his next strike, he saw Francine, his middle-aged blonde girlfriend, beckoning to him from the other end of the lengthy lounge. She had the telephone in her hand.

"I'll be back in a couple of ticks," he said. "Keep her nice and hot for me, buddy."

"Sure thing," smiled Sebastian drowsily. He had plenty left in reserve. Feeling her grow wetter again, he gave Dolly a long series of hard upward thrusts. She shut her eyes and once again visualised Pauline's sculpture. She lowered her arms and moaned.

Bernie walked over to Francine. She breathed out the smoke from her cigarette.

"What?" he asked.

"It's that caller from ten minutes ago," she replied. "Just rang again."

"Who?"

"Pauline. She wants some advice a.s.a.p."

"Fuck. What's the matter with her now?"

He took the phone from her.

"Better talk next door," said Francine quietly, inclining her head towards the adjoining kitchen. "You don't want Dolly to know what's happening to her darling Annabel."

Bernie handed her the crop and went into the kitchen with the phone.

"How you doing, Paulie?" he said, concealing his irritation.

*"Fine. How's my Little Dolly?"*

"Brilliant, just brilliant. We've given her a lovely all-over body tan. She's having a whale of a time. How about you?"

*"I'm good. But I want some advice about your knock-out powder. I've given it to Annabel and she's out cold."*

"How much did you give her?"

There was a pause.

*"The whole lot."*

"The whole lot? I told you *half*, Paulie, not the whole bloody lot!"

*"She's a strong girl. I wanted to make sure she was totally out before I start fucking her. I don't want her coming round on me while I'm still working her over."*

"Let's hope she comes round at all, for fuck's sake! I don't want another waste disposal job, Paulie. Not with this woman. She's too respectable. A hospital doctor. It's too bloody risky."

*"Don't worry, I'll take care of this one myself. She's my Special Girl, as I told you. What's the best way of bringing her round later on if I need some help?"*

Bernie sighed. He was troubled by what he was hearing.

"Try injecting speed, straight into her vein with a sharp." He glanced at his watch. "Don't leave it too much past midnight."

"*OK. Thanks.*"

"And Paulie – just a *small* amount of the stuff. Don't give the poor girl a heart attack! I'd like a stab at her myself when you're done with her."

"*Understood. Thanks for the advice, Bernie. Have a great time with Dolly!*"

There was a click on the line.

"Crazy fucking bitch!" he muttered, shaking his head. He handed the phone to Francine and took back his crop. He returned to the lounge, where Dolly was now riding Sebastian in a frenzy, her eyes tightly shut, groaning loudly and galloping hard to the finishing line. She bounced wildly up and down, her little breasts quivering, while Sebastian's cock made wet sucking sounds as it pumped faster and faster into her pussy. Her plastic ear-rings flapped about like big red butterflies. Bernie was suddenly aroused. It occurred to him he could assert his power over the girl by arresting her orgasm. He felt his cock surge into life.

"OK, buddy," he said, as he moved up to Dolly. "Just stop for a second…"

Sebastian abruptly stopped. Dolly gasped and shuddered to a halt. Her glazed eyes opened wide in surprise and dismay. Bernie grabbed the long dark pigtail at the side of her head and turned her face towards his circumcised penis, which was now fully erect. Forlornly, she looked up at him. There was a big malevolent grin on his face. With his narrow eyes and sharply cut beard, he looked just like the Devil. She knew how much he was turned on by her submission. She closed her eyes again, opened wide her mouth and obediently allowed his rigid cock to slide all the way down to her throat. As she sucked it and ran her tongue along the underside of it, she could already taste the approaching semen. If Annabel was Heaven, she thought, this must be Hell. But maybe this was where she really belonged.

What woke Annabel with a sudden rush was the odour of vaginal fluid – the uniquely acrid discharge that comes with a woman's orgasm. She could smell it over her face, taste it in her mouth. She knew it was someone else's fluid. Her face was pressed into a cushion. She turned her head and saw polished timber floorboards... discarded clothes were strewn untidily over them... grey skirt, blue blouse, black shoes, white socks and a petticoat... rolled-up nylon tights... a black leather G-string beside a jumble of dark green fabric... She saw a goat's head high on the wall looking down balefully at her... A large oak coffee table had been drawn up alongside her... on the table was a round glass mirror covered in lines of white powder and various tablets... next to it lay a couple of syringes and a plastic tube filled with fresh blood... she surmised it was *her* blood. At the end of the table was a heavy, expensive-looking camera with a big zoom lens... As she gradually came to, she realised that she was lying face down on Pauline's sofa, completely naked. For some time she was numb and unable to move. As she finally adjusted one of her legs, a pain shot through her backside, so sharp it made her cry out. She was sore all over, but especially down below. Her pussy and her bottom burned like crazy. She felt as if she'd been scratched and bitten every-where. Her heart was beating in fast irregular surges, and she was hot and sweaty.

"How do you feel, darling?"

Pauline was standing over her, also naked. Despite her pain and confusion, Annabel was fascinated: she had never seen her adversary's nude body before, and was curious to do so at last. She gazed at the long sleek pale figure, wiry and muscular, set against the splendid red hair; but her attention was quickly drawn to the heavy black tattoo on the white belly, stretching from the shaved pubic bone up to the chest, culminating between the small tight breasts. Each nipple was pierced with a zig-zag silver lightning bolt. As Annabel stared at the tattoo, Pauline smiled down at her.

"To answer your question, it's a depiction of Typhon, the ancient Greek dragon. *To Megalo Drako.* The devourer of souls. Vulgarly known as the Devil. My adopted deity. A very fine rendition, don't you think? I love the way the tail coils all the way down to my gash. There are some talented tattoo artists in this corner of London."

Annabel tried to speak but just groaned in response. Her face muscles felt weak.

"I know," said Pauline, sympathetically. "It's hard to say anything coherent after taking that stuff. It's a beefed-up version of Rohypnol – and faster-acting, as you found out."

Annabel looked up at the clock on the wall. It was a quarter past midnight.

"You've been out for over three hours," said Pauline. "I was beginning to wonder whether you'd wake up at all. Anyway, congratulations. You've just had your forty-first sex partner!"

Annabel looked at her again. Pauline held a thick white harness belt in her hand, now unstrapped from her waist. From the belt, attached to it, hung a smooth black phallic-shaped dildo, almost a foot long. Pauline moved it down towards Annabel's face. It was covered in lubricant and streaked with blood and brown mucous. Annabel recoiled sharply.

Pauline laughed.

"What's the matter, darling? It's the fruit of your very own loins, after all…"

Annabel groaned in despair. Now she knew why she felt so sore.

"I did promise I'd fuck you, Annabel, and that's exactly what I've been doing for the last few hours. With my little magic wand here. Well, actually, it's not so little. It was nice and smooth in your well-drilled cunt, but I have to say it was a *very* tight fit up your jacksie. Good thing for you, really, that you were out cold. And a good thing for me as well. I'd never have had so much fun with you struggling and fighting all the way through the proceedings."

She laughed again and wiped the dildo up and down Annabel's back.

Annabel whimpered. She felt nauseous. Fortunately there was nothing in her stomach.

Pauline continued.

"They call it rag-dolling – when you play with a totally limp and lifeless body, as if it was a corpse. I've been rag-dolling you, Annabel. Just like I used to with my favourite doll when I was a little child. It's what I always wanted to do with you, even when we were at school. Now I've finally done it… I've achieved my ambition! After so many years of waiting! But it was worth it. I've never had so much pleasure in all my life. Not even with Dolly."

The mention of her name roused Annabel.

"Dolly?"

"Yes, Dolly. If I know Bernie and Sebastian, they've been fucking her brains out over the last few hours. Of course, they don't need a dildo. They have real live cocks. And all kinds of whips and paddles to play with. Believe me, they know how to use their equipment!"

"You promised me…"

Pauline nodded, still smiling.

"Yes, darling, I did, and I'm going to keep my promise. After today, Dolly is all yours. And you're all hers… what's left of you!"

This confirmation brought some relief to Annabel. But her backside still hurt like hell. She moved her hand back and tried to pull aside one of her buttocks. She winced. Even this action was painful.

"I'd leave that area well alone, Annabel. Your arse has been well and truly deflowered. I don't think it'll ever look quite the same again. Never mind – you'll have a permanent souvenir of your time with me, darling!"

Annabel made no response. Annoyed by this, Pauline suddenly grabbed the dark brown hair and yanked Annabel's head up. She leaned down and looked close up into her face. Annabel could now discern the smell of her own vagina on Pauline's sneering mouth as she spoke.

"You see, *Jamey*? You're a victim after all! A pathetic loser, just like Dolly! The two of you deserve each other!" She spat in Annabel's face.

Annabel had guessed that this moment would arrive at some point. She ignored the spittle and smiled serenely back at Pauline.

"I'm glad to be a loser. Just like Dolly! It happens to us all. One day *you'll* be a loser too – darling!"

Pauline slapped Annabel's face, so hard that the sound seemed to resonate around the lounge, then angrily pushed her head down onto the sofa cushion. She moved over to the coffee table and reached for the curled up banknote lying next to the white powder. As she crouched to snort more of the cocaine, she looked over at Annabel, who was now lying motionless on her front, her face buried in the cushion. Still she was unbroken. And still she was beautiful, even when covered with welts and scratches.

"All right, bitch," muttered Pauline under her breath. "I'll show you what losing *really* means! I'll break you once and for all!"

She got up and left the lounge. Annabel was relieved to hear her go. She relaxed and drifted off into a light sleep, although she could hear Pauline moving about in a nearby room. Despite the cruel abuse and punishment she had taken, despite the pain throbbing everywhere from her face to her feet, Annabel felt a strong sense of… *accomplishment*, as if she had now succeeded in her mission to be the heroic sacrifice, paying the price to set free her lover. Her earlier notion had been right. This was something she had always needed to do, as part of her spiritual evolution. A line she had always needed to cross. Now, for the first time since she had been a child, she felt completely in touch with every part of her being. She was completely *herself*. Strangely, the pain and the pleasure had become one and the same. She dozed contentedly, still drowsy and exhausted by the drug…

She woke to find Pauline standing above her, still naked. She was holding a towel and seemed relaxed and solicitous. There was a slight smile on her face. She held out a hand.

"Come on, darling. It's time to get cleaned up. You're a total mess. After you've had a shower, I'll call a taxi to take you home."

Annabel took her hand and tried to get up from the sofa. But as soon as she stood up she became weak and giddy, and Pauline had to put a supporting arm around her back and under her shoulder before they could move towards the shower room. Annabel winced as she walked; her bottom throbbed painfully with every step she took.

Pauline paused directly in front of a full length antique mirror fitted to the wall and allowed Annabel to examine herself. Her body was soaked with sweat and covered with red marks of all shapes and sizes, mainly scratches and bites; on many of them tiny spots and lines of blood had risen to the surface of the skin. She could see puncture marks on her forearms, from which blood had been drawn. One of her nipples had been pierced by a needle and was swollen and twisted out of shape; a thin trail of blood, now dry, streaked down from it and almost reached to her navel. Both breasts had been extensively scratched and bitten. The gold crucifix still dangled over them.

Annabel moaned in despair at the sight of herself.

"Do you want to turn round and see the rear view?" asked Pauline. Mournfully Annabel shook her head.

"Good idea," said Pauline. "You wouldn't like what you'd see."

Annabel looked at her torturer's face in the mirror.

"Why, Pauline? Why?"

Pauline paused. Tenderly she drew Annabel close to her. She gazed at their image in the mirror as she replied.

"Because, Annabel, this is what we've *both* wanted – you as well as me! This is why you came here tonight. Do you understand now?"

Annabel looked at herself being held by Pauline, as if it were some-one else's body, and let out a long sigh. Then she slowly nodded, and smiled with an expression of weary acquiescence, watching her reflection nodding and smiling in weary acquiescence back at her. Now, in her dazed and disorientated state, she *did* understand. In the mirror the crucifix seemed to glow with a golden nimbus as she acknowledged her most secret and deep-rooted childhood desire. Her bitter adversary had brought her the fulfilment she had always craved.

"A true mortification of the flesh, Annabel! Saint Margaret the Virgin Martyr is proud of you! Your carnal sins have been well and truly expiated. Now you can take your place at her side. As Saint Annabel the Martyr!"

Pauline laughed out loud and Annabel noticed that her teeth were discoloured with dark red flecks. It dawned on her that Pauline had been consuming her blood.

"Now come with me, my darling."

Pauline led her away, and at the end of a narrow passage they came to a flush wooden door, old and heavy, which had been painted pitch black. It was the shower room.

As they entered the room, which was hot and brightly illuminated by round neon lights set in the low ceiling, Annabel thought that she was suffering visual distortions, an after-effect of her drugging. The area ahead of them was a long rectangle, some eight metres deep and three metres wide. There was no window and the walls looked as if they were made of dark grey polished marble. There was nothing inside apart from a large shower enclosure, which occupied the far end of the room from the door. The effect was dramatic and claustrophobic.

"What a shower room…" breathed Annabel.

"Yes. Impressive, isn't it?" replied Pauline.

She led Annabel towards the enclosure, which was formed very simply by two black marble side panels, set about two metres apart, which reached to the floor. There was a shallow base, likewise made of black marble, with a very large drain grill. The square steel shower head was the largest Annabel had ever seen: it was suspended by rods from the ceiling and covered the whole of the enclosure. On the wall were supply pipes and a control knob. With Pauline's help, she stepped in. She was still shaky and the marble floor felt very hard and cold. The grill dug into her feet.

"Steady now… I'll give you some support," said Pauline softly.

Annabel turned to face front and felt something slip onto her wrist; then it was slowly raised up towards one of the side panels and held there. Pauline promptly did the same with her other wrist, which was raised towards the opposite panel. Annabel, facing the length of the room, arms stretched out wide, suddenly realised that she was shackled to the two panels by handcuffs, which had been fastened to thick metal rings set deep in the marble, about five feet up from the ground.

"Pauline…" she said, perplexed, "what are you doing?"

"As I said, darling," smiled Pauline, "you'll need some support to get a proper shower."

She stepped back to inspect her handiwork. Annabel pulled at the cuffs, but there was hardly any give. She was held securely to the solid rings in the panels. Now she grew alarmed.

"I don't need this to have a shower. What are you doing?"

"Annabel – you're going to get a shower like none you've ever had before."

Annabel pulled harder at the handcuffs, to no avail. Adrenaline was waking her up quickly.

"This is ridiculous... let me go!"

Pauline shook her head.

"Sorry, darling. I can't. This is the final instalment of the price you have to pay."

"Oh God… surely I've paid enough already?"

"I thought so earlier. But I was wrong. We're going to need something more… *radical* to finish the job."

Annabel kept pulling, then stopped when she realised it was hopeless to try to escape from the cuffs. She started breathing quickly. She noticed that Pauline's eyes were larger and more glazed than ever before. She looked as high as the psychiatric patients that so often turned up at the hospital.

"I've had every last bit of your body but it's not enough," said Pauline, her voice rising. "I need your soul as well, Annabel!"

"Pauline, please! This is crazy! Let me go!"

Pauline shook her head.

"I can't let you go. Not after all the work it took to get you into my hands. All the months of careful planning!"

"What planning?"

"The planning that Dolly and I did, right from the start."

"Dolly? What do you mean?"

Pauline laughed.

"Everything was carefully worked out, my darling. The meeting with Dolly at the School Reunion Party. The meeting with her at the Gallery. The little note she handed you. The way she turned up at your flat after leaving a party so conveniently close by. Can't you see? It was all planned by us!"

Annabel shook her head, refusing to accept what she was hearing.

"Dolly was the bait and you're the catch, Annabel. She deceived you from the beginning!"

"No, no! Dolly *loves* me!"

"Oh yes, she loves you all right. She's completely infatuated with you. That's why she was the perfect bait – she was so desperate to have you! I chose her because she looks like you. She even dyed her hair the same colour as yours. And you fell for it big-time, darling! You fell for everything! Now you're in my net!"

"Oh God… this is insane!"

Pauline's eyes were bulging. She became more serious.

"Annabel… you don't understand. I'm not jealous about you having Dolly. I'm jealous about Dolly having *you*!"

Annabel stared back at her. Now she was wide-eyed as well.

"What are you saying? What are you saying?"

"It was always about *you*, Annabel. Right from the start, it's always been about you. You're all I've ever wanted!"

Annabel watched in amazement as Pauline pushed her fingers under the long mane of red hair and in one movement lifted it off her head. She threw the massive wig to the floor. Underneath it, her domed head was entirely shaven. She peeled off her false red eyebrows and finally stood there completely depilated. Her long white body and the stark black dragon tattoo gave her the look of an alien from a science fiction film. Her protruding ears and her big staring eyes, fixed on Annabel, added to the frightening effect.

"Oh fuck!" gasped Annabel. "What *are* you?"

"I'm your true love, Annabel! No-one has ever loved you more than me!"

She stepped forward into the shower enclosure and put her arms around Annabel, who had now given up struggling against the cuffs. Pauline's face was almost touching hers.

"From the time we were at St Margaret's, I've adored you like no-one else!"

Tears began to run down Pauline's cheeks. She caressed Annabel's back as she held her.

"Oh Annabel! You were my captain, my hero, my Miss Perfect! The only thing in my life that really mattered! You were everything I wanted but could never have… you were everything I wanted to *be* but couldn't be! Everything I've ever done has been to please *you*, Annabel – to make me worthy of you!"

Annabel groaned and shook her head.

"Why didn't you tell me? Why didn't you *say*?"

"Because I was never sure of myself. I couldn't be. Because I'm not beautiful like you!"

"Pauline – what use am I to you now? Look at me! Look what you've done to me!"

"None of that matters. I'm going to turn you into something wonderful – something immortal! Something perfect!"

"Oh God! What are you going to do?"

Pauline took a deep breath. Her bald white head gleamed under the bright neon lights. She pressed herself hard against Annabel's mauled body.

"I'm going to bring us together, my love. At long last, you and I are going to be as One. Together for all time! We'll *both* be perfect!"

She reached for the shower controls behind Annabel, who looked up at the colossal steel head above her. There seemed to be thousands of spray jets in it, all pointing down at her. She looked back at her captor, wide-eyed.

Pauline was euphoric.

"Prepare for the Abyss, Annabel! Prepare to meet Typhon!"

As if in a trance, the women looked long and hard into one another's eyes. Annabel now knew that she was going to pay the full price for the one she loved. For Dolly. The hero was going to be sacrificed. It was her destiny... as she had always known it would be. And now she was ready. She breathed in deep and felt the weight of the crucifix on her chest.

Pauline turned the shower control knob, all the way. The supply pipe hissed like a serpent.

Annabel closed her eyes, sighed, and surrendered to her fate.

The jets burst into life above them with an explosive roar.

The water came crashing down onto Annabel like the violent rainburst of a thunderstorm, and as it struck her body her first thought was that the storm-monster from the tennis court had come back for her and this time was going to take her. Then there was no more thought, just the agony of the freezing cold onslaught of water blasting down onto her body, going all over like searing acid, its iciness burning everywhere into her skin as she screamed out loud.

"Aaaaaaaaaaahh!!"

Every nerve in her body came shrieking to life at the same time, and it was as if an electric current ran through every last part of her. At once she began twitching, like an epileptic having a fit, her arms, her legs, her back, her breasts, her hips, her abdomen, all bursting separately and variously into a spastic life of their own. There was no chance of resistance or courage or self-possession, just the awareness of crazy jerking and twisting and thrashing in every direction at once as the freezing water attacked everything she had at the same moment without respite, relentless, merciless, terrible, her shoulders, her head, her chest, her belly, her buttocks, her thighs, her knees, awful, ferocious, overwhelming, her arms, her breasts, her back, her face, all control gone, agonising burning freezing terrible cold oh God no please, so cold, all going haywire and crazy no respite oh terrible freezing cold so powerful it hurts so bad oh fuck it burns like acid everywhere at once going all over the place no control just jerking twitching legs and arms and belly and arse and thighs and calves and feet and arms and shoulders and face and neck quivering aaaah God freezing must try to survive but how? where? hands tied high up can't get away oh fuck I can't get away, I'm losing it everywhere all over shaking and shuddering and arms twitching legs twitching I'm burning like acid oh God it's terrible, aaaah can't stand it, can't take it, aaaah it's too strong too heavy too much no chance oh God help me please stop it stop it please....

She was no longer aware of Pauline holding onto her... she was alone in the shower... one of her toes had pushed down so hard it was stuck fast in the drain grill.

I'm done, aaaah God, can't stop it burning jumping arms legs back twisting jerking oh fuck no it's so cold no chance help me God please aaaah please someone stop it aaaah too much can't take any more aaaah please God no I can't, every last bit of me oh God Dolly I'm sorry I can't do it oh help me stop it please it's terrible my body's going crazy all over everywhere aaaah I can't stand it anymore aaaah Dolly I can't do it.... all gone, I'm done, Dolly I'm done... aaaah God... aaaahh... can't take it..... aaaaaah....

Her self-awareness faded and she became nothing more than the nerve ends of her body, hundreds of them jumping and thrashing separately without concern for each other or for any other part of the body, just a complete anarchy and cacophony of reactions... all she could see was water, all she could hear was the blast of water coming down on her, all she could feel was the burning iciness numbing her skin, which was starting to lose all sensation, as if the skin was slowly dying around her trembling quivering body...

Time came to a standstill and she was just a cold carcass twisting and quivering without control or direction or purpose, just swaying numbly in the water storm as it came endlessly down on her, just swinging from the handcuffs like a block of frozen meat... More and more feeling drained away and the agony ceased as she felt her insides chilling and numbing and coming to a halt... there was no longer any sensation on the outside of her body... her skin was numb, was dead, like a sheet of ice, and there was no more twitching... just water pouring down down down onto her limp body... her flesh and her muscles were dead, her bones were frozen like bars of ice and her heart slowed down to a crawl... it couldn't pump anything through the icy block that her body had become... couldn't breathe properly ... her innards had now turned to ice. Everything stopping, nothing working any more, nothing living any more... everything frozen stiff... everything stopped... hanging limply from the walls like a frozen corpse... a big lump of frozen meat... no breath... just hosed down by the endless torrent of water from above, just pouring down down down on her forever... endless water... water... water...

Suddenly it was over. Her chest expanded sharply as her lungs involuntarily swelled with air, and her eyes rolled up hard into her head. There was a moment's pause. Then her mouth gaped wide open, her jaw dropped all the way down and she let out a long hard gasp. She felt herself sweep forward with the outbreath, as if she herself *was* the outbreath, and left behind the frozen carcass and the cold and the noise as she moved lightly forward into the curtain of water...

The curtain parted and she found herself in a silent airless place she thought must be the North Pole... it was the top of the world, the very summit of the world... it was the nearest place to the thousands of bright stars that twinkled in the clear inky-black night sky above her head. In front of her was a desolate snowy desert, the flat white land stretching away into infinity. It was a bleak endless plain with no life apart from her. She looked at herself and saw that her body was perfectly white and smooth, with no hair anywhere; she surmised that even her head was hairless. All colour had been drained from her. She had been completely stripped down and burned into a pure white essence.

There was nothing to do but walk forward into the distance, as far as she could. As she moved ahead, she noticed that the stars began to fall from the sky, one by one, and as each star fell the land darkened slightly and she lost a little strength. She carried on walking for as long as she could, but as more and more stars fell and disappeared, the plain ahead of her contracted and her energy drained away. At last so many stars had fallen that she could see hardly any white land ahead – everywhere around her had become covered in blackness, and she had no more strength left to keep going. She sank to her knees. The stars in the sky continued to disappear, one after the other, and after a few moments she allowed herself to fall slowly to one side and lie on the ground. The blackness was now closing in from every direction. Only a few stars were left above her. She rolled onto her back and looked up at the sky. There was no fear, no doubt, no struggle... she was content to give herself completely to the blackness... she knew that this was what she had always wanted, from the beginning... the resolution of all things. She opened her arms wide, held them straight out at either side, opened wide her legs, raised her knees, and waited calmly to be taken. The last remaining stars fell away, one by one, and the blackness came down and circled around her, closer and closer, descending over her from all sides like a vast endless ocean. Then it swallowed her, softly and silently, and as she finally lost herself and became one with it she realised that the blackness was infinite… everything and nothing… always and forever…

Everything and nothing

Everything

Nothing

Pauline stood in front of the tall antique mirror and was exhilarated by what she saw. She was the epitome of St Margaret's School, dressed immaculately in navy blue blazer, sky blue blouse, grey skirt and knee-high white socks. The flat black shoes were too small for her, and badly pinched her feet, but she was prepared to put up with the discomfort in order to wear the complete Form Captain's uniform. She really looked the part now, having put on the shoulder length dark brown wig with the centre parting and eyebrows to match. She breathed deep with satisfaction, and slowly, deliberately undid the top three buttons of the blouse. The white bra was much too large for her, but she loved the feel of the lacy cups against her chest, and the feel of the straps over her shoulders and across her back. She moved her hands down and pulled up the grey skirt to reveal the white silky petticoat slip, fringed with fine lace at the hem several inches above her knee. Then she raised this to admire the tan-coloured tights and the white cotton knickers underneath, which fitted her so snugly under the pressure of the nylon hose. She loved the sensation of the knicker-elastic pressing on her buttocks, the gusset held so tight over her crutch. Gently she fingered herself through the nylon and the white cotton, so that she could feel her pussy absorbing the inside of the gusset. What blissful intimacy! A wave of pure joy swept over her. She smiled and dropped the petticoat and skirt, brushing them back into shape so that she looked the impeccable Captain once more. At long last, *she* was Miss Perfect! Pauline Annabel Barrie… the Golden Girl of the School. Someone to be desired and envied by all. She was a winner at last!

She was distracted by the sound of sporadic dripping from the shower room. Obviously she hadn't fully turned off the control knob. It was a reminder that she needed to get on with her work – *the* Work. Her Masterpiece was finally at hand.

# XII

## LAST INTRUSION

IT WAS THE LAST DAY of August, late in the morning. The weather was still warm and humid but the sky over west London was now covered with thick heavy white clouds. A slim pale-faced young man, dressed in grey workman's overalls and carrying a tool-bag, turned unhurriedly from Warwick Road into one of the elegant Victorian streets that comprise the residential district of Earls Court. After five minutes he arrived at the address he sought, one of the many tall spacious red-brick townhouses in the area which had been divided into flats. He ascended the steps of the round-arched porch and applied a key fob to the panel beside the front entrance door. There was a brief buzzing sound followed by a click, and he pushed the door open with his tightly-gloved hand. He went in. He walked briskly up the stairs to the second floor and found the door of the specified flat. As usual, the communal lobby was deserted. He applied two keys, both on the same ring as the fob, to turn a mortice and then a Yale lock, and the door opened easily. He checked his boots again to ensure that they were clean. Then he entered the flat and silently closed the door behind him.

Quickly the intruder took in the details of the interior before starting his work. Everything looked tidy and normal. In the lounge he noted the large television and thick Persian rug, the profusion of books, records and CDs, the hi-fi stack, the colourful paintings and posters on the walls; but none of this interested him. He made for the small bedroom, which functioned as a study. On the sizeable desk was a computer, a few textbooks, numerous files and a pile of paperwork. He dropped his bag and started searching through the drawers of the desk, taking great care to damage nothing and leave everything in its original position. After a few minutes he realised that what he wanted wasn't in this room.

He moved to the large bedroom. The duvet was strewn across the double bed and the under-sheet was heavily wrinkled. On it lay a discarded t-shirt. A pair of crumpled gym shorts and fluffy slippers lay on the carpet at the side of the bed. The intruder leaned down and lifted the heavy mattress at both sides; he shone his torch to check underneath, but there was nothing. He stood up and looked around. The dressing-table was covered with cosmetics and make-up materials, plus an empty coffee mug. Next to it was a wicker basket full of used socks and underwear. Then he saw that the door of the large wardrobe was hanging open, exposing the full-length mirror on its inside. He pushed aside the skirts and dresses on the hangers and started searching the interior shelves. He knew this was a common place to hide things. Sure enough, under a pile of woolly jumpers on the highest of the side-shelves, he found a thick white envelope, unsealed. He removed it and pulled out a burgundy passport. On the inside back page was the photo and the name of the owner: Annabel Maria James. Yes, that was the one... He dropped the passport into his tool-bag. Also in the envelope was a slim wallet, containing several banknotes in Euro currency. This went into his bag as well.

The intruder had now obtained the main item requested by his client, but he wanted to find the additional material as well. He walked over to the bookshelf in the corner of the bedroom and saw it contained a number of hefty folders. Over twenty of them. All photograph albums. Helpfully, they were dated on the spines and arranged in chronological order. He removed the folder covering the period the client wanted, and out of curiosity put the album on the bed and opened it. The first page displayed the neatly hand-written title *St Margaret's 1977-79* and beneath it the subtitle *Golden Years!* Beneath this was drawn a delicately curved heart, and in the centre of the heart a perfectly shaped crucifix. Carefully turning the thick shiny pages with his gloved fingers, the intruder noted that the subject of the many photographs was the same person as in the passport, but of course much younger. The album featured pictures of her with one or more school-friends, aged from fourteen to sixteen, laughing or posing humorously in classroom and playground, in tennis gear, as members of a hockey team, doing athletics, dancing wildly in a disco, dressed up for a part in the school play, out on a school trip in the countryside… Occasionally there was a shot of her alone, close up, and she certainly was a looker. Lovely dark flowing hair, gorgeous smile… and a smashing figure. The intruder wished he had time to find out more about her, but he didn't. He closed the album and put it in his bag. He zipped it up. He had got everything he'd come for.

After a final check, to ensure nothing else had been disturbed, the intruder left the bedroom, walked across the lounge and made his way out of the flat, quietly locking the door behind him. As before, the lobby and stairwell were deserted. Nobody had noticed him. Another job done. But this one had been dead simple, as he hadn't even had to break in: the victim's own keys had been provided by the client. An easy day's work.

As he walked back towards the tube station in Warwick Road, he keyed the client's number on his mobile phone and waited for the recorded answer to finish. Then he left his message.

"Spider-Man to Typhon. All paperwork sorted. Delivery this afternoon as agreed. Bye now."

# XIII

## PAST PERFECT

Dolly turned into the narrow waterlogged alleyway that led to the Black Sun Gallery. She was in a foul mood. With the arrival of September, the summer weather had finally broken and a never-ending slew of rainclouds had filled the sky to spoil her holiday plans. She hadn't heard from Annabel for four days and was feeling rejected. Pauline had been late in paying her and she was now flat broke. And she was sore all over. She had to wear a long-sleeved top and black tights under her denim hot-pants to hide the purple marks and the bruises that covered her body after the party at Bernie's place. Well, today was the unveiling of Paulie's latest work, the sculpture she claimed was going to be her Masterpiece. It was a good time to turn up and sort things out.

She went into the entrance lobby. Sebastian smirked at her from behind the desk. He was still full of himself after the party.

"Hi, Little Dolly. Feeling a bit under the weather today?"

"Fuck off, Sebastian. Is Paulie here?"

"Whoa!" Sebastian shrank back in mock-fear. "Yes, darling, she's inside. They've put her new exhibit in a special room on its own. It's rather big, I have to say. See you later…"

Dolly tossed her long hair back over her shoulder and strode into the brightly lit main gallery, which still accommodated Pauline's "Superreal Women" exhibition. A few spectators were wandering about as usual. There was a sign at the far end of the gallery displaying the title "Past Perfect" and an arrow pointing towards a side room. She walked directly up to the sign and saw that the side room was crowded with people, some twenty or more, all milling about and chattering. There was a real buzz of excitement. Something big was going on. She could see a huge glass cabinet of some sort in the middle of the proceedings. She caught a glimpse of Pauline's flame red hair and decided to go in.

After a few seconds the crowd in front of her thinned and Dolly made her way to the exhibit. Suspended above it was a large sign, heavy black lettering on a white background, which read "Past Perfect". She gasped when she saw the work. The glass cabinet, over ten feet long, lay at waist height and was shaped like an old-fashioned six-sided coffin, broadening out widely at the shoulders, and it contained a fully life-sized crucified figure, lying horizontally. The cross was made of glossy polished black steel girders, which had been neatly formed into a crucifix. Nailed to it, lying on its back, was a beautifully shaped woman's body, entirely nude, made from what looked like smooth shiny white silicon or resin, as hard and impervious as a shell. As Dolly peered through the glass, she was astonished to see that the supine figure looked exactly like Annabel. It was a perfect resemblance, just like the rendering of her own roller-skating pose that Pauline had used for the "Girl's Destiny" sculpture. But this looked even more impressive. The size and proportions of the body were so *absolutely* like Annabel's, it was uncanny. The figure was completely shorn of hair and lay with arms outstretched and knees raised, opened wide and sharply bent, to bring the feet up high on the black girder, to within only a few inches of the buttocks – a provocative touch typical of Pauline. It looked almost as if the crucified woman was about to give birth. Dolly manoeuvred herself past other viewers to reach the foot of the cabinet and saw that the legs were open wide enough to display in full the shaved vagina. She was surprised to see that the chubby lips looked exactly like Annabel's, although the folds of inner labia had been cut away to make the whole thing look smooth and tidy. The anus had likewise been smoothed away. The hands and the twisted feet were pinned down by large thick glossy black nails, at least six inches long, which had been hammered in deep and hard. There were even patches of dark dried blood at the points where the nails drove into the white resin. The effect was quite brutal. The head lay back so that the face looked up at the ceiling. The pupils of the eyes were painted black to show that they were crossed and rolled up into the head, and the mouth gaped wide open in an ecstatic rictus, giving the clear impression of an orgasm brought on by the crucifixion. This was a really blasphemous touch. Amazing! Looking at the whole thing, Dolly found herself getting turned on. It was just like watching Annabel climaxing in bed, legs apart. She was really missing her…

"Sweetheart – there you are!"

Pauline walked up to Dolly and gave her a big kiss. She was obviously in a good mood: the exhibit was a huge success. She was dressed in a full length black gown and, oddly, wore a hefty gold crucifix around her neck.

"Hi, Paulie. Wow, this thing is fucking brilliant! It really is your masterpiece!"

"Thank you, my love. I must say it's been a big hit."

Rickie came striding up behind them. He was effusive.

"Pauline, this work is absolutely superb! I'm going to do a special piece on it in next month's edition, with reference to the triumph of de Sade in the New Millennium. Can we talk about it later?"

"Of course, Rickie. I'll catch up with you in a little while."

"Just out of interest, is it based on a Life-casting? I assume it must be. It's so naturalistic." He stroked his beard as he gazed at the figure's wide open vulva. Other spectators strove to catch Pauline's answer.

"Yes," she replied. "A good friend of mine agreed to model for me. The sculpture is a hard-core base coated with fibreglass and resin. Makes a nice smooth finish, don't you think?"

Rickie nodded vigorously. "Yes, yes, it's truly exquisite. OK, see you later Pauline. And you, darling." He winked at Dolly, who made no reply, and left them.

"Huh! What a jerk!" snorted Dolly.

"Yes, but a very useful one," smiled Pauline. She waved at another journalist she had just seen.

"Paulie, what's with the crucifix? You haven't gone religious, have you?"

"No, Sweetheart," she laughed. "It's just to promote the exhibit. Nice antique piece, don't you think?"

"Yes, very nice. I like the carved figure."

"Well, I think I'd better go and see a few people…"

"Paulie, can I just ask you… how did it go the other night with Annabel?"

"Oh, it went fine, darling. Just fine."

"Did she… fulfil her part of the deal?"

"Absolutely. She gave me everything I wanted."

"So that's why she agreed to model for this work?"

"Yes. That's why."

"So I did everything right… to deliver Annabel to you, as we planned from the start?"

"Yes, you did everything right. You've done exactly as I wanted. I'm very grateful."

"And you didn't tell her I helped you?"

"No. I didn't."

Dolly was relieved. She paused before asking the big question.

"So... does that mean the deal between you and me is now agreed?"

Pauline put an arm around Dolly's shoulders and smiled benevolently.

"Sweetheart, I can promise you I'll stick to my part of the bargain. You're now free to go whenever you want. Your debt to me has been paid in full."

Dolly's heart jumped with delight.

"Thanks, Paulie. I really appreciate that. You're a straight dealer all right."

Pauline paused. She looked pensive, and gazed down at the glass cabinet.

"Somebody once told me that's the nature of love – that there are no strings attached. She was right."

She now became a little despondent.

"Dolly, I think it's best that you leave me anyway, and turn over a new leaf. Start again somewhere else. As it happens, I've just incurred a sizeable debt myself."

Dolly was confused.

"What sort of debt, Paulie?"

Pauline smiled wistfully.

"The greatest debt that any person can possibly incur. I recently overplayed my hand in a very expensive game."

She saw the puzzled expression on Dolly's face.

"In fact, I may be called upon to repay the debt very shortly. It's best that you're out of the way when that happens, Sweetheart."

"I don't understand, Paulie, but I hope you'll be OK."

Pauline kissed her on the cheek and prepared to move away to the journalists who were waiting to interview her.

"One last thing," said Dolly. "When can I get to see Annabel?"

Pauline frowned.

"You may have to wait some time, my darling. Annabel has decided to go away for a while, to escape from the hoo-ha surrounding this latest exhibit. She doesn't want anyone to know that she modelled for it."

"But… she would have got in touch with me and told me what was happening. I've been trying to phone her for the last four days and all I get is her answering machine."

"Well, she may be away for quite some time, Sweetheart."

"Do you know where she's gone?"

Pauline shook her head.

"Far away from here. Where no-one can find her. I don't think you'll be seeing her for several weeks – maybe even months. But don't worry – you'll be fine!"

Dolly was stunned. Pauline touched her arm.

"Now I must go, Sweetheart. See you around."

With that, Pauline moved off and was immediately surrounded by a group of people.

In a daze, Dolly turned back to the exhibit and placed her hand on the glass cabinet. She felt numb. As Pauline's words sank in, her heart dropped like a stone into a bottomless void. Suddenly her eyes began to burn. She looked at her face in the reflection of the glass and was surprised to find it streaked with tears. She wiped her cheeks with the back of her hand but realised it was hopeless. Her face stared back at her in despair. And she felt that she would cry for the rest of her life.